# Young Wife Shared

## On a Desert Island

## Matt Coolomon

### Edited by S.H. Madonna

X-Rated

High level erotic content

Young Wife Shared on a Desert Island

First Cuckolding: Book 5

Copyright © 2013 Matt Coolomon

Independently Published

ISBN: 9781520281605

# Part 1: Plane-Wrecked

## Justine

"So, what happened to you today?" Adele asked me. She had taken the seat beside me in the small plane and left our young office assistant Steven seated across the aisle. He was peering over with interest. He was my husband Paul's cousin and had a serious crush on me. Paul was sitting up front beside Thomas.

"I just took a sick day," I told Adele. I wasn't about to get into what had happened. Paul and I had fought last night. We had watched a porno movie and started making love when his erection failed again. I had tried to tell him it was alright – that the doctor would figure it out. Paul's frustration had gotten the better of him, and he became abusive, taking it out on me. I had taken his car and spent the night at a hotel. I'd found him sulking at home in the morning, and we had spent all day talking and trying to get a handle on numerous small issues that had been coming between us lately. We made a booking to begin counselling.

"I just had a headache and decided to take the day off," I lied to Adele. I would confide later. Right then, I just wanted to sleep.

We were my father's office team. The Morris & Falkner Law Firm. We were on a small chartered flight to Tahiti for our Christmas party. There was Adele and her husband, me and mine, young Steven and the two lawyers, old Thomas and Mr slick, Jasper Morris.

Jasper was always in a finely cut business suit. His short, dark hair manicured to perfection. His teeth brilliant and his constant smile and steady green eyes making my heart thump every time he turned them on me. Which was often. He was up front behind the pilot and chatting with him but the weather was a bit rough and the pilot was trying to concentrate on flying the plane.

An hour into the flight, I had dozed off when the plane suddenly lurched and plummeted for a few seconds, then it started jolting and there was an explosion visible through the windshield.

The pilot was gripping his controls and anxiously yelling 'mayday mayday' into his microphone. Everyone was screaming, and I just clung to my seat, still in the grip of my nightmare.

The plane plummeted through the lightening and driving rain. It swooped down and banked left, then there were trees and the crashing of timber, and I was thrown forward then reefed back and all was black.

I came-to with my vision gradually clearing to focus on Jasper's bloodied face. He was different. The arrogant smirk was missing, and in his eyes was pure shock and terror. At last something genuine from the guy, was what I was thinking. Though I wasn't really thinking. My brain was mush and I had no idea where I was or what was happening.

"You all right, love?" Thomas asked me. He was his usual caring self. He was examining Paul's leg, which was bloodied. Paul grimaced as Thomas ripped his trousers open up to his knee.

"I'm all right," I told the older man. I could see a tree a few meters in front of me. I remembered I was in a plane, but so too was the tree, it seemed.

"Is he alive?" Thomas called out.

"He's breathing." It was Jasper again. He seemed to be taking charge. Did he mean the pilot?

Across the aisle, Steven was coming-to. He was bloodied but appeared okay. The fuselage was ripped open along his side of the plane.

Steven looked at me, but he was in a daze. There was blood dripping from his forehead down his nose. There was a gash in his right shoulder with flesh exposed through his shirt.

"There's no fire," Jasper announced. He had crawled back from the cockpit to face us other four conscious survivors. "Check out the first aid kit... can you bandage these two while I try and find the others?" he said to Thomas.

Thomas agreed. Jasper climbed out through the back of the plane and was gone. I turned to watch him and found that there was no *back of the plane.*

"Where's Adele?" I screamed. The plane was missing from where Adele had been sitting with her husband. After we chatted earlier, Adele moved from beside me to sit with her husband further back.

"We don't know," Thomas said to me. "Half the plane's missing and we don't know."

We were suspended off the ground but not too high to jump down. The storm we had flown through was gone, and the forest was in sharp moonlight.

I found the world around me spinning until the moonlight faded and my nightmare ripped me from consciousness completely. I came-to again to broad daylight. I was being carried by Jasper. He stopped and put me down as I started struggling. I walked along for a while, but my head was still spinning, and I ended up being carried again.

I saw a small cabin and was taken inside and laid on a cot where I drifted off into unconsciousness once more. I had picked up bits of the conversation between the men and understood they had seen the cabin from the plane and decided to find out what it was and maybe get help.

When I awoke the next time, it was evening and the men were sitting at a crude wooden table in conversation around candlelight. "Where are we?" I asked them. My head was clearer than before and I remembered most of what had happened. "Where's Adele?"

Thomas approached. "Adele and Ronald didn't make it, love. The pilot too."

I cried, and my husband pulled me close and comforted me. I sobbed into his chest until gaining some composure to face things. "So where are we?" I asked weakly, feeling sick from the horror.

No one knew. They all shrugged. Jasper spoke. "We don't know where we are, Justine. This looks like some sort of weather research facility. There's some charts and books in the corner. There's a heap of supplies in those cupboards, so who knows what goes on here."

There was no communication equipment, and Jasper had climbed back up to the top of a ridge that afternoon while we had all rested. "I couldn't see anything but trees and ocean," he explained. "It could be an island. I'll explore some more in the morning."

"We were flying for over an hour. We could be a thousand miles off the coast," Paul added. "There are hundreds of small Pacific islands."

"But what about beacons and that – don't planes have something for when they crash, so they can be found?"

"Yeah maybe," Jasper agreed. "We don't know. The pilot was out to it, and we don't know what the go is with that."

"We just have to wait," Steven offered with concern. His head was bandaged and his arm was in a sling."

"Are you okay, Steve?" I asked, approaching behind his chair and leaning there. My head was aching but not spinning anymore.

"I'm okay," Steven said to me and offered a smile. "Are you?"

"My head's thumping," I declared. "Are you okay, Paul? How is your leg?"

Paul was sitting on the arm of a couch. His lower right leg was in a rude splint. "I don't think it's broken," he told me.

"It could be a fracture," Thomas added. He went to one of the cupboards and pulled out a box with a red cross on it. He opened it and found bottles of pain killers. He handed out two each to me, Paul and Steven. Jasper brought us a glass of water to share.

"I think we should eat," Thomas declared. "There's canned vegetables and meat."

Us survivors spent the night warm, dry and with full stomachs, at least. The next few days Paul, Steven and I recovered while Jasper trekked in all directions and Thomas kept house and played doctor. The cabin was only a half a mile from the beach. In the opposite direction it was about the same. It appeared to be a small island and completely uninhabited with the only sign of civilisation being the cabin and a satellite dish mounted on a ridge not far away.

I had a problem with clothing. I had recovered my bag from the plane crash but only had a party dress with shoes to match, and some panties. I was going to wear the dress without a bra. For the flight, I had worn a short floral house dress and my raincoat over that. Underneath, I had on white lace panties but no bra. I didn't have a bra at all, as it was. I had intended to buy a new bikini for the weekend. I hadn't been planning for an indefinite stay on a desert island. At least I had worn my tennis shoes, though.

# Paul

I usually liked it when Justine went braless at home. She was washing dishes, wearing a shirt I had given her so she could wash her dress. The shirt covered her panties, although it sometimes opened at the bottom and flashed them. Her nipples were erect right then, pressing against the light-blue cotton fabric, her tits with a slight jiggle and sway that showed they were unfettered.

Jasper was watching her do the dishes as well. He was rocking back in a kitchen chair, staring distractedly. I saw his gaze lower to my wife's legs as she reached up to a cupboard, the shirt lifting to almost reveal her panties at the back.

I felt my face flush a bit and my heart quickened. I couldn't blame the guy for looking. I'd been out drinking with Jasper a few times. He was always checking out women. I quite liked him, though it was weird with Justine around, half naked, as she was.

The guy is an alpha, that's for sure. That's how I see him when we're doing shit together. He's got that confidence and arrogance about him and I haven't really. I've always known he checks out Justine at work but it's like I'm supposed to let him get away with it somehow. Like he's almost a bit envious of me with such a hot wife. Which makes me feel good about myself, so I guess I kind of want him to look at her.

That was all in my head right now. Not so much rationalising it, but getting a kick out of the alpha trying to perv on my wife.

Justine collected Jasper's plate from in front of him and wiped the table with a cloth. His gaze lowered down her shirt. There was one button open at the top and he was looking in through there. I tilted my head to see my wife's cleavage. She wasn't showing any nipple, but the view down the front of the shirt revealed the full roundness of her tits.

She just blushed and flashed a glance from the alpha's ogling eyes to me and away as she went back to the sink tugging her shirt over her bottom. Jasper just smirking and making me look away to avoid challenging him at all too.

This became commonplace as the days passed. My wife would either be in her short frock or the shirt, no bra and sometimes even without panties, although she was noticeably guarded when completely bare beneath. One afternoon she had fallen asleep on her cot. Thomas was in the cabin with her. I came in from the veranda and found her with her legs tucked up and her pussy exposed from behind. I tugged the sheet up to cover her.

Thomas shrugged apologetically. "I didn't know whether to do that. I've been trying not to look."

I had known Thomas for years. He was a nice old guy, not at all sleazy. "I might put up a curtain to give Justine some privacy," I told him.

"That's a good idea. There's some shade cloth we could use," Thomas suggested, and that afternoon he helped me partition off a room for my wife.

# Justine

There was an abundance of supplies, but after a week with no sign of a search and rescue mission, it was decided that stock should be taken of what we had to make do with, in case it needed to last a long time.

"Well, who knows how long? It could be months, even years!" Jasper warned.

"I still say whoever uses this cabin will be back in June. That logbook shows they're here every June through September," Thomas surmised.

"But even June is six months," I declared. "How are we supposed to live here for six months?"

"On rations," Jasper said practically. "We need to plan this and we'll be fine. There's fishing gear. I hope we all like fish," he said and grinned. He was actually settling into the situation better than us others. He seemed to be in his element, I had noticed.

As far as food went, there was enough canned fruit and vegetables for the five of us to survive on for six months. The cabin had 12 small bunks, and seemed to have been stocked for that many people. There was plenty of soap and toilet paper. There was coffee, tea and dried milk. There was some wine and beer, but not much. It would have to be rationed sparsely.

Jasper went on, "If we plan for six months that would be one beer for each of us men every couple of days, and, Justine, you could have a bottle of wine every now and then?"

"Suits me. I don't want any beer," I agreed.

"You guys can have my beer," Steven offered. "I don't really drink unless I'm out with the guys."

"Well, there's the half carton of cola, you can have that," Jasper offered. "And that's about it for the luxuries."

"Um, can I have the razors?" I asked, trying a sweet plea to get them. There were only a dozen or so disposables. "You men could just trim your beards with scissors, couldn't you? Please?"

The men all laughed. "Yeah, better to have a hairy chin than a hairy woman," Jasper said.

15

I replied just as confidently, "Well, no one's *having me* but I'll be easier to live with if I'm allowed to remain presentable and semi-civilised."

"Well, *having you* in terms of your fine company is what I meant," Jasper shot back, glancing at my blushing husband.

I couldn't help being turned on a little by the way Jasper dominated my husband. Especially here on a desert island with no one to police the matter at all and stop Jasper from simply taking me.

*Oh my god, stop thinking like that Justine!*

The razors were placed in front of me. We had decided to divide the things in short supply. It would be easier to ration them if we each had stock to be responsible for.

"I need that cotton wool," I said, blushing a little. "I don't have anything for that time of the month, and it looks like these people must be all men."

"There's some things in Adele's handbag," Thomas said. He got it from the corner of the cabin where things from the plane had been put. "I haven't looked in her other bag," he added as he handed me the handbag.

16

I found a packet of tampons and a couple of panty liners, and stashed them with my things. I wondered what clothing might be in the other bag. I wouldn't be able to wear the dead woman's underwear, but there might be something else. Any bra would be too big, anyway. Adele had been quite busty while I'm only a D-cup.

"Clothing is the other problem. I might have to use one of the sheets to make a skirt or dress or something. All I have is this frock and Paul's shirt and my party dress," I said.

"Yeah, it's the same for us, love. There's no clothes here, and we've all only got what we were going to wear for the weekend." Thomas pulled something from his things and handed it to me. It was a white singlet. "That might be a bit revealing but you can have it."

"Oh, thank you!" I cried, holding it up against myself. It was long enough to be a dress, though the arm holes were almost down to my waist.

"It'll be a bit loose beneath your arms though, love. Do you have a bra to wear beneath it? We noticed you haven't been wearing one so far."

"I didn't bring one." I blushed. "You men are going to have to promise you won't stare when I'm wearing it is all. Although I feel like a bit of a native anyway."

"I'm going to wash a couple of things right now if anyone wants to throw something into the tub. Save on soap," Jasper said. "You got anything, Steven?"

"Yeah these," Steven said, getting his shorts from his kit. He also brought a singlet. "You can have this too, Justine. It needs a wash first, though."

"Oh thank you, Steven!"

Thomas tossed some underwear into the wash tub. "That singlet's clean if you want to wash your dress, love," he said to me.

"Oh okay," I replied and I ducked behind my partition.

I came back out with my nipples visible through the white singlet and the darkened patch of my pubic hair also visible. The hem came well below my crotch, so I was covered in that regard, but my breasts were on display from the side. It was far more than I would usually dare to show in public.

"Hmm this really is revealing, isn't it?" I said.

18

"Looks better on you than on me," Thomas laughed.

"Hell yes!" Jasper agreed, making me giggle.

Paul was frowning from his seat across the table. I sort of shrugged apologetically, but again it was thrilling somehow to be looked at by these other men in front of him. I was enjoying the stares while tugging at the singlet to keep my nipples covered.

"But we can see from the side," Steven said with concern.

I blushed. "Well, as long as you don't get any ideas!"

"No new ideas, just the ones I've already had being enhanced," Jasper tried playfully. "Sorry, Paul… the only girl in town though."

"Yeah right," Paul said, shaking his head in defeat.

"Well, you'll just have to take care of those urges yourself," I told Jasper, giving a mock glare.

"Yeah, but for a whole six months?!"

Everyone laughed. I did too but I was thrilled to be the only female in the room and on the entire island. With four strong virile men!

I took on the task of washing and started kneading the clothes in the tub. The big singlet gaped forward slightly. I looked down at myself and rolled my eyes at the men. "So, this is why you gave me this, hey Thomas? And I thought you were being chivalrous."

"Justine, we can really see a lot!" Steven said again.

"Well, there's not much I can do being stuck here with all you men and with hardly any clothes to wear, Steven. I've seen each of you getting changed a few times already. There's not much any of us can do about it."

"There's actually room up in the loft if you want us to move your cot up there," Jasper offered. "It would be a bit more private for you."

His eyes lifted from my breasts as he spoke. I blushed a little when he glanced back down and up again. I met my husband's gaze and plucked at the singlet again, adjusting it to keep my nipples covered.

"I don't mind my room where it is if one of you guys want the loft," I answered. I liked sleeping amongst the guys and wasn't moving anywhere.

"I'll have it," Steven said.

The other men agreed, and Steven climbed up. Jasper went outside and Thomas helped Steven lift his cot up the ladder.

I approached my husband and cuddled him as I stroked his head. "Sorry, but I don't have anything else to wear. There's nothing I can do about it," I whispered.

"But we can see your tits from the side, darling. We can even make out your pubes through this. Jasper's loving it. He's checking you out big time."

"But it's not his fault we're here, in this situation. He's been great. And he's always checking out women. It's not just me... except I'm the only one around at the moment."

"Yeah well, it's hard to watch. It's not so bad with Thomas because he's an old dude, and Steven's trying not to look."

I kissed my husband's forehead. "I know, but it works the same both ways. They've got no privacy here in the cabin at all, and they've even given me some of their clothes." I thought for a moment before going on. "Actually, I don't feel uncomfortable at all. There's something kind of primitive about being here like this. I don't actually mind being semi-clothed like a native girl. It doesn't seem like the big deal it would be back home."

"Yeah, I suppose." Paul grimaced as he shifted his leg.

I gave him two more pain killers then went out to hang the washing. Jasper brought firewood to restock the pile beside the cabin. He sat on the step, wiping his face on a towel.

"So, those are your only underwear?" he asked, keeping his voice low. He was looking at the panties I had hung on the end of the wash-line. He spoke sympathetically. "Could you cut up a sheet and make something."

"I've got no cotton or a needle to sew with. I could make a dress or skirt. I could make something to wrap around my top," I responded practically. "I have another pair of underpants, fortunately."

I did have another pair of panties but wasn't wearing them right then. It was exciting discussing the matter with Jasper. I felt so naked under my singlet and my pussy was tingling wildly, my belly too.

"I think you're right about having to just relax and accept things with us having to all live together. And we're all friends," Jasper went on. "Plus, you're a married woman."

"Hmm, I don't know how married I am here on this desert island. There are you four men and I'm the only female. That's all I can think," I argued, blushing at the thought and fiddling with the hem of the singlet.

He tilted his head, looking at my thighs. I glared and scolded him. "Don't!"

I was trying not to giggle though and he was smiling. "It's okay, I've seen it a few times already," he assured.

I just blushed deeper and shook my head. "It's not an *it*, thank you very much!" I scolded some more.

"No it's a cute little pussy. Nice smooth lips thanks to the razors, eh?"

Oh this was so wrong but god I loved talking about my pussy with this man.

"Well that first razor is already getting blunt, so don't expect too much," I defended, like the guy was entitled to expect me to show him.

"It's not about expecting, more so appreciating," he said and looked up from down there as I turned and resumed hanging the last of the washing.

# Jasper

I had always enjoyed the fact that Justine was a married woman. At work, it was kind of naughty checking her out, knowing she was spoken for and off limits. I was looking at her upper-thighs, enjoying that she had nothing on beneath the singlet. She tugged at the back of it, as if reading my mind or feeling my eyes.

"Are you still going up to the satellite dish today?" she asked me.

"Yeah, just about to head off."

"Can I come? I'm tired of being cooped up here."

I immediately imagined climbing up the mountain trail behind her, getting flashes of her cunt.

"Sure, you can come. It's a bit of a climb though." I grinned. "You going to wear just that?"

She blushed, smiling and shaking her head. "You're hopeless, aren't you?"

"Yeah. Can't help myself."

"Hmm I guess! But I think I'd better put my other undies on."

Justine was at the bottom of the steps with the washing basket. She edged past and glanced down as I watched her thighs and nearly glimpsed what I wanted. She returned after a moment with her tennis shoes and sat on the step to put them on.

I leaned to the side to look up her make-shift dress. She glanced at me, blushing a little. I watched her thighs until they inadvertently parted and I saw her panties. "Ooh, there they are!" I grinned. "Covering your girly bits though!"

"Well, I *am* a girl," Justine giggled back at me.

"That you are," I replied more seriously, and I took her hand to help her up. "You know, I wouldn't wish being stuck here on anyone, but I'm very glad you're here... you being a girl and all, with girly bits."

She responded to that after a moment, also being serious. "I know what you mean. I'm glad to be here with you men. It's nice being the only female, and sort of flattering."

I led the way for a while, climbing up the rocks first and pulling Justine up by the hand. We reached a point on the trail where there was a wall of rock with a ladder bolted to it. It was only a short climb, about four metres. I took Justine's hand again, but that time I ushered her forth to go up first.

I grinned. "You got this?"

She blushed again, biting down on her smile and shaking her head. "Okay, but they're as good as bikini pants, you know?"

She gave a final, defiant glare and climbed the ladder. I leaned in underneath her and had a look at her little white panties cutting into her cunt. She looked back down at me. "Damn glad you're here, baby!" I grinned up at her, and she giggled.

When I gained the level of the rock ledge with her, she pushed my shoulder playfully.

"I can't believe I just flashed you like that. You're such a pervert."

I looked at her chest. Her nipples were erect and prominent through the thin singlet. The white roundness of her breast was visible through the armhole. My cock was straining against the restriction of my shorts.

I adjusted it. "Gave me half a woody."

"Sorry," the girl uttered.

"I'm not."

She smiled through a deepening blush. "I mean, I don't mean to tease you. I know what men are like with their needs."

"What needs are those?" I asked with mock innocence.

She rolled her eyes and led on up the trail with me following behind. It was another climb up a rocky knoll, and as Justine scaled the first rock I had another nice view of her from behind. She has slender thighs, so it was actually quite easy to see her crotch.

She peered back blushing and smiling, and she tugged at the singlet, trying to cover herself a little.

"I think you had better lead the way," she said when I gained the level of that rock with her. "I might have to cut up one of the sheets and make myself a long skirt so you

27

men aren't being teased too much when there are no other women here to satisfy you in that way."

"Yeah, the old blue balls." I chuckled. "Not nice!"

"I know." Justine blushed. "I mean, I don't know! But I'm sure it must be uncomfortable in that way for you men, and you shouldn't be made to feel like that and have to – you know – like, for yourself."

I took her hand to help her up another rock. "You really feel that way?" I asked sincerely. "That's a nice way for a girl to look at it. It's very sexy."

"Sexy?" Justine giggled. "It's about *not* being sexy!"

"Don't think that's actually possible. Not for you, baby."

"Well, you men have to try not to think like that about me. Especially if we're going to be stuck here for ages. But you still have to take care of me," she added sweetly. "That's the other good thing about being stuck here with men. Feeling safe and protected."

We had reached a point that I had found earlier. "Here, you can see all the way across to the far coast from here. I'm pretty sure this is a tiny island."

I showed Justine where I had explored thus far. I had yet to travel to the south, but there were no trails, and the terrain was steep and almost inaccessible. If it wasn't an island it was a very narrow point of land that was entirely isolated.

We had approached the small timber building with the satellite dish mounted above it. I had busted the lock earlier. Inside the building was electronic equipment that appeared to be some sort of weather measuring gear. It meant nothing to me, and there was nothing that looked like it could be used for communication in any way.

"See, this is all that's here," I was saying.

I climbed up a ladder to get on the roof of the small building where there was a further view out to the ocean to the north, east and west. The cabin was also visible down in the thick forest. Justine appeared beside me with the wind blowing her hair all over. She gathered it while I looked at her tit through the armhole of her big singlet. I could see the roundness of the underside. Her nipple was high-set and visible through the thin fabric. She was busy looking out to sea, and she kept her arm raised to hold her hair.

She suddenly turned and caught me looking before I glanced up. Her arm dropped and she folded it across her chest. "Hey you!" she scolded.

"Sorry. Couldn't help it." I grinned, glancing down again.

She punched my arm playfully, so I grabbed her around the waist and tickled her. She squealed and laughed, squirming but also clinging to my arm as I held her. Fuck she felt good to get hold of. Her tiny waist and warm soft tits resting upon my arm.

"Don't!" she protested, still giggling.

"What, no tickling allowed either?"

"Not up here, it's too scary," she pleaded.

I was getting an erection from holding her. Her bottom was pressed back against me, and just the feel of her tits as I kept my arm lifted up against the underside of them.

Of course she's a married woman though. I needed to try to respect that a little bit. Her husband was no problem if it came down to it, easily handled if he wanted to go there at all. But I had to respect her wishes until she gave enough indication that she was open to me going further.

"Are you scared of heights?" I asked, releasing her.

"Little bit. Except it's a nice view up here, isn't it?"

"I think we should make a *help* sign there in the clearing in case a plane flies over. Maybe another one down on the beach," I suggested.

"Uh huh, although I kind of hope we don't get rescued too soon. It's actually not so bad being here," Justine said wistfully, looking out to sea again.

When we were ready to leave, I offered her the ladder first, earning a small blush, and I just had a look at her tits from above. I also led the way down the rocky trail and helped her in places.

At one point Justine had to virtually sit and slide down a smooth rock with me ready to catch her if she slipped. She watched my face with my eyes focused on her panties. Her singlet had bunched up, and they were fully exposed to me that time. I caught her, clutching her bare skin above her waist. I tilted my head to look at her panties some more before she tugged the singlet down.

She met my eyes and grin with a warm blush. I grabbed her again as she tried to walk past. My fingers dug into her ribs, and she giggled and squirmed to get away.

"So, we're allowed to tickle you, eh?" I asked, lunging again, but she ducked clear that time.

"I don't mind being tickled sometimes, but not my legs," she tossed back at me. "I can't stop from squealing when guys tickle my legs, and I might accidentally kick you if you try."

"Where on your legs, your knees or up higher?"

"Never you mind!" She giggled. "Anywhere above my waist is fine but not my legs!"

"*Anywhere* above your waist?" I asked pointedly.

She glared back at me, but I lunged again and almost caught her. She ran to the ladder and climbed down, smiling up at me as I watched from above. When I climbed down, she waited for me.

"No more tickling now, okay?" she said, reaching up to rake her hair back into place.

I looked at her tits. Her nipples had been firm all the while. "Okay, no more tickling for now, but is everywhere above your waist ticklish? What about here?" I asked, kneading her shoulders. "You're not ticklish there, right?"

"No, not there. That just feels nice."

"And what about here?" I went on playfully feeling her back and digging my fingers in enough to make her flinch and squirm.

"Um, yes, a little bit there," she said.

I smoothed her hair to one side and breathed on her neck. "What about there? That's above your waist."

"Um yes, but that's not exactly the same kind of ticklish," she uttered.

I placed my hands upon her waist and looked down over her shoulder. I lifted my hands a little. "And what about those cute little tits, they ticklish?" I whispered.

"Sort of!" she said, clamping her arms to her sides and stopping my hands from lifting further. "Are they really little?" she complained.

"They're perfect. They look fantastic in that, and in that dress you've been wearing with no bra."

"Really?" Justine uttered. She still had her arms clamped tight and had folded them beneath her breasts, but she wasn't covering them.

"Yes, really!" I said warmly. "They look good from the side in that, and the way it shows your nipples. And the way your dress is kind of loose fitting and shows us a nice look at them when you lean forward and that. I mean, big boobs offer lots of cleavage, but with nice sized ones like yours, we get to see your nipples down your dress sometimes from the right angle, which is damn exciting for a guy."

Justine blushed back up at me, biting down on a smile.

"You don't mind us getting little flashes, do you?" I grinned cheekily.

"Hmm." She pushed away from me and led on towards the cabin. "You're typical men, so I guess you can't help looking," she tossed back at me. "Plus, I've only got this and my dress and a shirt to wear, anyway."

"Yeah, and you don't need to make any long skirts. It's nice how short that is on you. You've got nice legs."

She smiled back again. "Thanks. As long as I can keep them shaved, though."

"Sounds fair. You get all the razors and we get to look at your legs."

We had reached the final step down from a small ledge where I had gone first and waited, looking up at Justine. I held my hands ready to guide her. She slid down to me with my hands going under her singlet to claim her bare waist again. I also gathered her in my arms that time and carried her across a small trickle of water with her singlet still bunched up and her panties fully on display.

"Thank you, kind sir," she uttered as I placed her down.

"You're welcome, pretty lady." I winked, making her smile some more.

"Actually, I was thinking of one thing I could make from a sheet to wear. I could make a simple tunic. Just with a rectangle of fabric with a hole cut for my head and a tie around my waist. I could make about three of them from one sheet."

I smiled. "You could make them short, though?"

She rolled her eyes. "Yes, quite short!"

"And sort of narrow so we still get to see from the side?" I tried cheekily, tilting my head to have a look at the exposed side of her tit again. "If you made something that was open all the way down to your waist, we'd have a nice view all the while of the only titties on the island. And we men need to see titties otherwise we have withdrawals and go stir crazy. We really need you women to show them off for us."

"Oh, you do, do you?" Justine giggled. "But what about Steven, I'm married to his cousin! And Thomas is my neighbour and a friend of my parents! I'm sure they wouldn't want to see my breasts."

"Yes they would," I replied simply. "If we're going to be stuck here for months, young Steven is going to be desperate for contact with girls. At his age, guys don't think about much else. And old Thomas isn't past it either. Have a look at the history on his computer next time you're in his office. He's an old hound dog for college girl sites online."

"Really? Thomas?"

"Sure! He's only human. He needs it just like the rest of us."

Justine was quiet for a moment, seemingly thinking. "So, do you think I should talk to Paul about being really open with the way I dress, since I'm the only female? I mean, if you men need it, I guess it's something I could do to make it easier for you while we're stuck here. And I guess it would be only fair since I'm going to have you men taking care of me and making sure I'm safe."

"Yeah, we'll be taking care of you, baby. Young Steven's going to be doing the fishing to feed us. Old Thomas has settled into the kitchen."

"And you just make me feel safe," Justine added warmly. "Ever since the crash you've been so calm and strong. You make me feel like everything will be alright and this is just some crazy island holiday. You make it seem like something positive, not like we're stranded and lost."

She was quiet for another moment before continuing.

"So, maybe I should do what I can to make it nice for you men here," she said. "Would you really like me to not cover up too much? I'm still married, so I can't actually do anything – like, physically – but I can let you enjoy looking at me if you're sure it won't just make it worse to not have any women."

"Looking is better than nothing," I said. "It's far, far better than nothing."

Justine blushed. "Okay then, I'll talk to Paul about it tonight. Now that we've talked about it like this, I'll try to explain to him about us all having to share. And with me being the only female, he shouldn't mind you other men looking at me. He's been okay about it so far."

"Yeah, more nipples and more flashes of your cunt would be good, baby. That's what we need."

My blush fired up but I didn't look away. "Hmm, it's not called that either!" I scolded, stretching my singlet down in front defiantly now.

"Yeah it is, you've got a cute little cunt," Jasper teased, smirking and trying to grab and pull up my singlet.

I jumped clear, giggling. "It's not that… it's my vagina or my pussy, if you must!"

"Yeah well we need to see more of it, baby." The guy had caught me and held me from behind. "We need to see more of your pink little pussy and these perfect tits," he said and groped me before I managed to wriggle away laughing and hurry along the trail towards safety.

Oh my god I was on fire inside now though. I was the only girl stranded with four men on an island, and the alpha male was starting to demand what he wanted and get handsy with me!

I wished I had no panties on right now so I could let him see what he wanted.

# Paul

I watched from the window of the cabin. Justine had been gone with Jasper for a couple of hours. They appeared together coming from a trail into the scrub, both smiling and chatting as they walked. Thomas and Steven had gone to check out a fresh-water pond Steven had found. Jasper turned and took the trail down to the beach. Justine came into the cabin alone.

"Hello husband," she greeted cheerily, and she straddled my lap and kissed me. "Where is everyone?"

"Gone looking for fresh-water bathing. Steven found a pond."

Justine ground against my package. "Mmm what's going on down there?"

"Don't know." I met my wife's kiss and groped a breast.

"Wow, that feels hard. Do you want to put it in?"

"Is Jasper coming back?"

"He went for a body-surf. He'll be hours." She ground along the underside of my erection. "Wow, that's a full-on boner! Give me. Give me!"

I pushed my shorts down and she guided me in through the edge of her panties, swallowing me with her wet heat. I surged up into her, my cock harder than it had been in ages, and it was the kind of hard that was *not* going down before I got off. Lately I had been getting an erection but only a half-hearted one, one that I could feel was in danger of waning. The thought of which added to my trepidation and lack of confidence, ending things quickly.

Justine reached orgasm just as I did. We held each other tight and squished our soppy crotches together. I sought my wife's mouth and kissed her. I chuckled. "I'm cured."

She giggled back. "It seems so." She squirmed some more. "You're still hard, Paul. That's very impressive. You came, didn't you? It felt like you did."

"Yeah, I did. It just feels normal again. It's been so long, I could come again easily before this one goes down."

"Can we go to the bed? Is your leg okay for lying down?"

"Fuck my leg. I don't care about that."

Justine led the way, lying on her cot and pulling off her panties. I lowered to her and entered her again. I held the frame of the cot and screwed my wife through another orgasm before erupting deep inside her.

I got up off her and sat on my own cot, beside but beyond the partition. We had decided not to sleep together. Not to rub it in to the other men, who had no partners to cuddle up with.

"Oww!" I exclaimed. My leg was throbbing now. I put it up on my cot and rested back.

Justine was rinsing her panties in the wash tub. She came back and hung them to dry.

"Could you get me a glass of water please, sweetheart?"

She brought two glasses from the kitchen and lay on her cot, on her side, facing me. She was smiling huge. "Well?"

"Well what?"

"What happened? How come you can suddenly do it again?"

"I think it might be because you're so frigging sexy, sweetheart. This half-naked stuff is hot."

Justine bit a lip. "Yes it is, isn't it? It makes me feel sexy."

"As long as we're careful not to do anything with anyone around, I suppose."

"Uh huh definitely," Justine agreed. "Although, maybe we don't need to worry too much about being half naked with the others around."

"Yeah, I know. Like we said before, and I've been thinking about it. I'm cool with it now," I told my pretty wife. "You're getting around looking hot and sexy, and they can't help but notice. It's all good, darling."

Justine nodded. "Yeah." She was blushing a little. "Plus it's kind of fair, don't you think?"

"Fair? What the hell do you mean?"

"Well, just that we don't have much here. We're all missing out on plenty of our usual luxuries and things we enjoy. And maybe this is one thing I can do to make it a bit nicer for everyone. Since all three of those men are making my time here more comfortable, that is. I don't have much to offer in return as a weakling girl stranded on an island, but I know how much you guys like looking!"

I took that in. I swallowed hard. This was an interesting take on things. "You mean they should be entitled to look at you?"

"Well no, I'm sure they don't feel *entitled*... It's not like I feel obligated, but then again, they haven't been obligated to help us either. Steven's out all day fishing because he can do that to help. Thomas took care of us all when we were injured from the plane crash, and he's been doing all the cooking. And Jasper's been amazing."

"Yeah I guess," I agreed. "And as soon as this stupid leg heals, I'll be doing my bit too."

"I know you will. They all know that. It's just nice how everyone wants to do what they can to make it as nice as possible for everyone else." Justine smiled through her blush. "And I'm the only female, stranded with a bunch of men. Which means I could start being more flirty and making it kind of fun for everyone. Even for you, obviously!"

I had to shift my pants. My cock lifting.

"Oh my God, it's back again!" Justine cried, pointing.

"I know! The damn thing won't go down now."

"See? It's because you like the idea of me being flirty, don't you?"

"Yeah I guess."

The idea excited me. I didn't imagine anything different from what had already been going on. So far Justine had been inadvertently teasing the other guys. Acknowledging it and intending to continue was even sexier.

"I'll be cool about it, sweetheart. I won't get jealous or silly. As long as we can find more chances to fuck like that, I'll be a very happy man!"

The crudity earned a mock glare. I smiled it off cheekily.

Thomas and Steven returned with news of a nice pond for swimming and bathing. Jasper came from the beach and built the fire to heat the water for showers. We men all had a quick one, and Justine waited until after dinner, to let the water tank heat again. She spent half an hour having her wash.

She came from the shower wrapped in a towel and combing her hair. She had one of her razors in her hand. Her legs looked smooth. The raggedy green towel held above her nipples and just covered her crotch. Steven's mouth was open as he watched her walk by where he was sitting at the table. Thomas stood gawking from the kitchen. I was seated adjacent Steven. Jasper was the third member of the Euchre game. He turned to watch her squeeze past behind his chair. She poked out her tongue at him, smiling.

Jasper reached back and clutched her above the knee, making her shriek and jump back. "No! No leg tickles!"

she pled, holding a hand up to keep him away. She was giggling and blushing.

I was suddenly flushing hot too and my heart was pounding.

Jasper lunged and caught Justine's wrist. She squealed and he grabbed her ribs, getting his arm around her as she squirmed back against him. He clawed her sides, making her laugh and thrash about with her arm across her breasts, holding her towel in place.

"Damn, she's ticklish, eh?" Jasper said, glancing at me.

"Very!" I replied, my heart thumping hard as my wife was still being held by this other man.

She was regaining composure. Jasper lowered his arm from around her and lightly kept hold of her hip as she stood beside him. She resumed combing her hair, the towel almost lifting high enough to flash her panties. Or her pussy. I wasn't sure if she was wearing any panties. Her nipples were close to popping out the top of the old towel too.

"Can I play?" she asked sweetly.

"Take my place, love," Thomas called over. "Does everyone want coffee?"

Justine sat across from me. She had to constantly fix her towel as we played cards, each time attracting the gaze of all of us men watching on. I noticed the dark areola peeking above the towel at times but never the actual nipple. At one point, I rocked back in my chair and looked into her room to see one of her pairs of panties folded with clean washing and the other still hanging up to dry.

I imagined her sitting there across from me and between the two other men with her bottom bare on her seat and my cock sprung to life.

What the fuck was going on with this!?

She yawned and stretched, fixing her hair again and her areola were peeking again. The other three men were all staring and she just blushed and tugged up the towel.

"Oh yeah, nearly got them that time!" Jasper joked.

Justine giggled and just shook her head. "This towel is either too short down below or up top. It's not fair."

"It's really short!" Steven agreed worriedly and gulped.

"Works for us," Jasper teased and tilted forward for a look up it.

My wife looked to me. We met and held our gazes while the men chuckled and bantered. Thomas leant over to have a look up her towel too and she just blushed deeper and tugged at the bottom of it.

"Love that is awful short," he said. "Where are your panties?"

"Um, I don't want to wear them out washing them all the time."

"Uh I see," the older man agreed, nodding and tilting for another look.

"Is it teasing you too much?" Justine asked them all.

"It's impossible not to look," Jasper said flatly. "As long as we're allowed."

He tilted in for a deliberate look this time. I held my wife's eyes, her blush on fire.

"We are allowed. Yeah?" Jasper pressed, glancing from Justine to me.

I swallowed hard and nodded.

"Aw shit!" young Steven squeaked, his eyes boggling as he looked too.

All three of them were tilting to look up Justine's towel now. She smoothed the edges across her upper thighs and left it, just gripping the seat either side and with her tits straining at the top of the towel with the way she was drawing big breaths and expelling raggedly.

"Yeah that's nice, man. Looks wet," Jasper tossed back at me with a wink. "Lucky you eh!"

All four of us men were erect in our pants and shifting to adjust and make room.

"No, he's not getting lucky with you other men here and having to go without," Justine said and tugged at the top of her towel to cover her areola again. She also crossed her legs and tugged the towel down a bit to cover herself.

"Aw that wasn't long enough!" Jasper grumbled disapprovingly.

Steven was too busy crushing his erection to the side and looking worried to join in the chuckling and further banter. Justine ended up leaving us to it and went to bed anyway, pulling her partition closed to more grumbles of protest and glaring back at Jasper and poking her tongue out.

# Justine

I was indeed wet and absolutely on fire inside as I lay there listening to the men talk. I finally managed to sleep and didn't see much of the men at all until I returned the next afternoon from a walk on the beach. Thomas was visible sitting just inside the door of the cabin as I approached. He was reading a book.

"Where did you get that?" I cried. "Is there any more?"

"We found some more stuff up in the attic. There's girl's stuff up there. There must have been women staying here at one time."

"Girl's stuff?"

"Yeah, feminine products as well as some romance books. It's all there for you, love," Thomas said, indicating a box on my bed.

I rushed to it and found boxes of tampons, deodorant, some make-up and about a dozen books. "Yes!" I cried excitedly! I also found more razors underneath the other stuff when I tipped the box up.

"There's a big box of candles too," Thomas informed Jasper. We hadn't found many in the other storage and would have been running out fairly soon. "Enough to last ages," Thomas added happily.

"Can I have my shower now, please?" I asked Jasper, blushing a little. "Look! Deodorant!" I cried. "I need to wash and put some on."

Jasper went and set the fire under the hot water drum. It was a simple, gravity fed arrangement that sent water through a pipe system and heated it. A warm shower could be made quite quickly.

I came out and took the dry clothes I'd hung earlier back into the cabin. I returned with my towel and toiletries, and my other pair of panties in my hand.

I smiled. "Is it ready?"

"Should be fairly warm, not hot though."

I tested the water. "It's warm enough," I said.

The door to the shower opened facing the cabin. Thomas had come out and was sitting on the steps reading his book. Paul limped from inside and sat beside him. Jasper left the fire and went up onto the veranda to lean on the rail.

I was here to put on a show it seemed. I wanted to. I was ready for this now and had decided to tease the men as much as possible and even allow them to see me properly sometimes, like last night.

I closed the shower door and stepped out of my panties and took off my singlet-dress. Glared and smiled defiantly at the men grinning like fools.

# Paul

"You've got a beautiful wife, man," Jasper said to me.

I felt my skin tingle, my hair lifting a little at the open comment. "Thanks. And I guess I don't mind you guys noticing, under the circumstances."

Thomas smiled. "It would be hard not to, son. I've noticed you've been taking it well."

"Yeah well, we're all stranded here. Nature all around. Justine's turned into a bit of a native, is all."

Jasper grinned. "Yeah, favourite bit of the day, watching the native girl shower, eh Thomas?"

The older man chuckled. "They could have made that door a bit smaller."

"Yeah, that's true," Jasper agreed.

Steven appeared from around the side of the cabin with fish he'd caught for dinner. He put them inside and returned to the steps.

"Sit down! Enjoy the show," Jasper said to him. "Paul said we're allowed to watch."

He sat on a wooden chair on the small veranda. When Justine lifted her arm to shave, her breast was almost exposed above the door. We could see a portion of it but, again, not quite to the nipple. Then when she was washing her hair with both arms raised, her breasts were almost popping over the top.

"She's a married woman, though! She's my cousin in-law!" Steven declared.

"Yeah well, she doesn't mind us looking," Jasper replied evenly. "It's only natural for all of us men to want to look at her. She's the only female here, so what else are we going to do?"

"I guess," Steven conceded. "Are you sure it's okay, Paul?"

"It's alright, Steven. It's crazy being here like this. Nothing's normal."

"Well, I've always found it hard to look away from the girl, and now she's a young woman and we're here like natives and it's damn hot and she's got hardly any clothes to wear!" Thomas looked from Jasper to me helplessly. "I mean, her parents and I are the best of friends, so I really shouldn't be looking either."

"You just have to relax, the pair of you! These are extraordinary circumstances," Jasper said as he stood. He walked down the steps and went back over to stoke the fire. Justine was rinsing her hair with her arms raised and her eyes closed. Jasper stood from the fire chamber and fiddled with a join in the water pipe leading to the shower. My heart was thumping at what he looked like he was thinking. Justine was facing him, still running her fingers through her hair and with her head back and eyes closed.

"Oh my," Thomas groaned under his breath as Jasper lifted his head and had a look over the side of the shower stall at my wife. "But son..!" Thomas said to me and he gripped my shoulder.

I swallowed hard and glanced back at him just as my wife squealed and giggled. She had her arm across her breasts and was glaring at Jasper. He was chuckling.

"How's the water, is it getting hotter?"

"Yes, it's lovely thank you!" Justine had turned her body away and was smiling back over her shoulder while Jasper continued fiddling with the water pipe, which was actually leaking a bit. There was a wrench on a chain that was obviously kept there to tighten the fittings. Jasper knelt and worked one on the ground.

Thomas was still gripping my shoulder. "Are you okay, son?" he asked, giving me a firm shake.

I swallowed hard again and nodded back at him, catching young Steven's blank gaze as well. "He's just being himself," I said to them both, my face hot with a flush of embarrassment. "It's like he's been in charge here ever since we got stranded. He just um… you know, it's hard to say anything after everything he's done for... like all of us really!"

"Yes, but she's your wife," Thomas challenged quietly.

"Aw shit, he's looking at her again!" Steven warned under his breath.

I turned back to see Justine with her arm obviously across her breasts again, only she was still facing Jasper peering over the shower stall this time. He was motioning to the shower head and saying something about the flow of water from it. Justine reached up with her other hand and held it while Jasper tightened the fitting. He tilted his head and looked at her body. Justine peered back over her shoulder at us other men. She was biting down on her lip, her blush visible as she held my gaze and lowered her arm from her breasts.

"Oh son," Thomas groaned.

I just swallowed hard again and took a big breath. My wife raked her fingers through her wet hair, both arms raised and out of Jasper's way as he checked another fitting, his eyes fixed upon her.

Jasper looked across at me. My face felt hot as I held his stare. I felt Justine's eyes upon me too as she seemed to be watching the interaction between us men. Jasper had another deliberate look at her over the shower partition. She remained facing him fully with her arms raised and her hands in her hair. She watched him looking up and down her body, just chewing her lip and gazing at his face.

I almost wanted the guy to reach in and touch her. He did reach into the shower stall but only to tighten the main fitting a bit more. He smirked at her. "That water running a bit cold now eh?"

Justine covered her tits with her hands and glared defiantly. The guy chuckled and had a last lingering look over the shower stall at her before putting the wrench back and returning to the steps.

He glanced at the other two men then looked at me. "Hey," he said, his brows flickering as he smirked a little. "Been meaning to tighten those joins, eh."

I nodded and took another breath. "Yeah..."

Jasper winked at Thomas and looked back at Steven. "It's okay Stevo, she didn't mind."

"I think she's finished now," Steven said, looking from Jasper to where Justine was drying her hair with her towel.

She came from the shower stall with the towel wrapped around and all her clothing in her hand. The bottom of the towel was uneven, with one edge of it up to her bare groin and only a corner of the thing covering her pussy. She bit down on her smile as she approached where Jasper was leaning right back on an elbow smiling up at her.

"You have to let me through," she said to him as she held my shoulder for balance and edged between us. She had her handful of clothing clutched across her breasts, holding the raggedy towel up. Jasper was grinning and leant in under to have a good look up between her legs. She just shook her head blushing and held her hand over her bottom as she walked up the stairs.

Jasper gave her a quick pinch up under the towel and she shrieked and spun around pushing at his hand. She was laughing and trying to back away but he had hold of the bottom of the towel.

"Get out of it, meany!" she scolded him.

She had hold of the bottom of the towel herself, clutching it defensively, but her other arm had lowered inadvertently and one of her tits was uncovered and shuddering and jiggling bare as she laughed.

Thomas and Steven's eyes were on her tit. Jasper was tilting under and looking at her pussy. She kept backing into the cabin and he crawled along after her until she was inside and he was halfway through the doorway too with us other three craning to see what was happening.

Justine shrieked again and darted for her partitioned room while Jasper ended up triumphantly waving the towel at us.

I edged past him and went to find my wife hiding behind her partition and pulling on a singlet. I grabbed her and kissed her hard, felt down over her belly and found her slick and so damn hot inside when I inserted a finger.

# Thomas

When we all went inside, Paul and Justine could be heard talking softly behind the curtain. I started on dinner and Jasper and Steven played cards at the table. It was getting on dusk and we had candles set around the cabin after deciding how to ration the new supply to last the anticipated six months or so.

Justine finally peeped out from her curtain. She met Jasper's eyes with a blush and looked at where Steven and I were. She slipped from her bedroom and approached behind where Steven was seated and hadn't seen her yet. Jasper looked her up and down, nodding approvingly. She smiled in response, rubbing down her body nervously.

"This one's a bit shorter, but it's still fine, don't you think?" she asked sweetly.

She had on the sky-blue singlet Steven had given her. It hugged her breasts and had her nipples hard and poking at it very obviously. It ended just below her waist, leaving the tiny triangle crotch of her panties exposed.

"This will be nice to wear after my shower and to bed. Does it look nice?" she asked us men.

We were all staring wide eyed. Paul limped over to the couch and fell into it, lifting his leg to a cut piece of log Jasper had brought in for him.

"It's very nice, love," I said to Justine. "It's all that you young girls sleep in these days, isn't it?" I looked at her legs then lifted my gaze slowly to meet her blush.

Steven gulped. "It's really short."

"But I don't have any shorts or a skirt to wear," Justine replied practically. "You gave it to me, Steven, and the only way I can wear it is like this, with my panties. Unless you'd rather I wrap a towel around or something? Or I guess I could make a wrap-around skirt from a sheet."

"I think she looks fine in panties." Jasper grinned. "That singlet's plenty long enough if you ask me."

Justine looked down at herself. "It's only the bottom bit showing. You can't see the lacy part up higher."

She turned to show us from behind. Her panties were high-cut bikini briefs. They were white. From behind, we could see her bottom hugged nice and tight and the thin strip of shiny fabric between her legs. She turned to face us again with the soft material cutting into her slightly and moulding to the shape of her smooth vulva. Steven was staring at the little white triangle.

"It's not like your family will ever know every detail of what went on here," Jasper said to the boy. "Don't you think Justine's nice to look at?"

Steven looked at Paul then at me, I'd approached from the kitchen. "I didn't know my singlet would be so short for you to wear though," he said to Justine.

"Well, I'll cover up if you really want me to," she said. "Do you want me to, Steven?"

"Aw, I don't know. I guess not really!" he answered, looking to me again. "I guess I've seen your panties before anyway," he directed at Justine, grinning a bit.

"Really! You little sneak!"

"Yeah a few times around the house," he went on proudly.

There were two leather lounge chairs. Justine sat in one with a book she had picked out. She tucked her legs up and to the side. Her little panties were then stretched up tight, and with her slender thighs, the full crotch was visible to us men. She smoothed her hand over her bottom with the four of us staring.

"Don't worry you look good like that. Very sexy," Jasper said to her.

She smiled. "Thanks. Though I'm the lucky one. I've got all you guys taking care of me and you've only got one girl to look at a little bit." She smoothed her hand upward and uncovered the back of her panties more fully. "Is that better?" she said teasingly.

"It's a nice shape over your girly bits. Cuts in and looks good!" Jasper offered, winking at Paul, whose face had heated slightly red.

"Well, like I said, I *am* a girl!" Justine giggled.

"Yes, we can see that, love." I chuckled. "Can see that quite clearly!"

Justine blushed. "Well, I should hope so. Sitting like this."

"So, did you see her in panties or just get a look up her skirt, Steven?" Jasper asked.

"Up her skirt," he answered.

Justine looked at him, but his eyes were focused on the back of her legs.

"Me too," I added. "I've had the pleasure of a few up-skirt flashes over the years."

"Well, at least this singlet covers me better up top than the other one," Justine said, plucking at the fabric. "At least it's nice and tight so it doesn't gape and show boobs. And it's smaller under my arms so you men can't see them from the side."

We were all looking at her breasts. "Still shows off your nipples nicely though," Jasper said. "Doesn't it, guys?"

Steven and I said nothing. We just kept looking at Justine's breasts while she peered up, blushing at us.

"You can only see their shape, though. Not like the white singlet where you guys can see them through the fabric," Paul said, shaking his head in defeat, it seemed.

He was grinning. We all laughed.

"So, you don't like my singlet, love?" I asked teasingly.

"Oh no, it's great! Thank you so much for letting me wear it. I really need it, and I'm going to wear it a lot, even though it's so revealing."

"You're welcome, love," I offered. "You're very beautiful... very sexy looking."

Justine smiled at me. "I'm glad you think so, Thomas. Thank you." I approached and sat on the arm of her chair as we were talking. She got up on her knees and gave me a hug. "I'm really glad you're here too, you know? I mean, not that I would wish for you to be stuck here like this, but since we are, I'm so glad to have you here making me feel safe… I mean all of you men of course. I've got four strong men to take care of me and I want you all to know how much I appreciate that."

"And we appreciate having you here too, love. We all do, don't we, Steven?"

"Shit yeah!" Steven added. "I'm so glad you're here, Justine. I wanna do anything I can to make it nicer here for you."

"And so do I, for you men," Justine uttered, looking to her husband. "If I can make it so you don't have to be completely without women, to enjoy looking at, at least. That's why you don't have to pretend not to look at me or anything. You can all just enjoy looking at my legs and at my chest, like you guys always want to with girls. You don't have to worry about my parents finding out, Thomas.

65

And you don't have to worry about your parents finding out, Steven. I won't say anything about it when we get back."

She finished up still on her knees on the seat of the chair with her arms up while she raked her hair back. Her singlet had lifted to her belly with her little white panties completely exposed. Jasper and Steven were sitting across at the table and both were staring at her panties. I was still resting on the arm of her chair and was looking at her breasts.

She held my shoulder for balance and peered from my face to the other two. She smiled through her blush. "But I get to look too," she said sweetly. "I don't have to pretend not to notice when one of you are taking your shirt off."

I laughed. I held young Justine's back lightly as she talked and smiled up at me. I was thrilled with the feel of her through the thin fabric of her singlet, and with the look of her nipples so firm and poking out like that. The fish was going to burn, though, and I had to return to my cooking duties.

I was absolutely thrilled to be stuck here on an island with my neighbours' lovely young daughter. I adored Justine, and had done ever since her family moved in next door when she was a child. I had adored her as an innocent little girl who was always over playing with my own children. I had appreciated her beauty as she grew into a young woman, as I had appreciated my own daughter's beauty. I had more of an eye for Justine as a young woman, though, as I was in fact not related to her. I noticed her sexuality and had to avoid her parents noticing that I was noticing!

Suddenly I was there, stranded on a tropical island with her, though. And she had virtually no clothes to wear. And she was saying it's fine to look!

***

# Part 2: Men in Need

## Thomas

I watched my neighbour's young daughter blatantly throughout the evening in that rustic little cabin where we were plane wrecked with barley any clothing to wear. I watched her around the island the next day and the next. I would sit on a seat in the sun staring at her legs as she hung washing or lazed around herself. I'd be waiting patiently for a flash of panty and she would just smile at me and teasingly swish her legs together or tug her clothing into place to cover herself.

She had made a tunic style dress from one of the sheets. She was wearing it while doing my beard. "This is so nice," I said.

"Well, I don't see how you can do it yourself when there are no mirrors anywhere. You can tell this place is a man's camp. You guys are hopeless!"

Justine had a small mirror in her makeup kit, but we men all jumped at her offer to do hair and beard trimming.

She was snipping away, trimming my beard as close as she could. When her arm lifted, I looked in through the side at her breast. The fabric was gaping away from her body and I could see the nipple. My eyes rolled up to meet hers. She was blushing and I did too.

"They're nice," I said, grinning. "Perfect size."

"Really? They're not too small?" she uttered. "Paul talks about me getting implants sometimes."

"No – no – don't do it, love! Don't even think about doing that to them. We're all loving them just the way they are. I can't get my eyes off them with you going braless here."

She giggled. "I noticed. It's fun being braless here with you guys, though. It's very flattering the way you all look at me, you know?"

"You make my old singlet and that sheet look very fashionable, love."

"What, this old thing?" Justine exclaimed playfully, looking down at herself and brushing at some beard clippings.

The tie around her waist needed adjusting, so she untied the knot and brushed more clippings away. While it was undone, I tilted my head to have another look in through the side. I saw both breasts fully and glanced up to meet her blush and smile. She had to re-thread the tie through some holes she'd cut in the fabric, and as she did that she inadvertently uncovered one of her tits.

"Yeah absolutely perfect," I said warmly.

She bit down on her lip, looking from her bare breast to meet my eyes. "Does this make it easier for you here or harder?" she asked softly. "I don't want to tease you and make you miss your real girlfriends even more."

I smiled. "I hope we don't get rescued too soon. Before we run out of supplies, but not too soon!"

Justine giggled.

"I noticed you don't close your curtain at night anymore," I said.

"No it's too hot."

"Hmm it is hot, isn't it? And humid."

"Yes, but the evening storms are nice," Justine said.

"They *are* nice. And you look nice when you're sleeping too, love. The way you kick the covers off and your little panties are always showing."

"Oh really! And do you watch me sleeping?"

"Not creepy like. It's just nice to sit up and see you there like that."

Justine nodded agreeably. "Well, I did think about it when I first decided to leave my curtain back. I thought you guys might like to see me in bed. Sneaky like!"

I chuckled. "We do, love. But how about sleeping topless for us sometimes? That would be nice."

Justine's blush deepened. She took a moment to respond. "I guess I could if you want me to. Just in the moonlight or candlelight, though. I don't mind you men getting flashes, but I don't think I could stay topless in broad daylight for you."

She stood before me fixing her hair back in a tie. The front of her tunic lifted to reveal the tiny white triangle between her legs as she did that. I looked at it. She had on the panties with the lace front. Both pairs were white and only distinguishable by the lace.

"Well, it's definitely easier being here with you showing your tits and panties, love. You make it very nice for us men."

"I'm glad." She smiled down at me. "I know how men are very visual, so I think when a man takes care of a woman he should be allowed to enjoy looking at her body."

She bent to kiss my cheek, whispering softly, "So, yes, I will sleep topless for you, but my parents really can never find out about any of this, okay? It would be weird for them with you being their friend and knowing that I've been undressing for you."

Justine kissed my cheek again then took her broom and dustpan up to the loft to tidy Steven's room. She had taken on housekeeping as her share of the chores. She blushed down from the top of the ladder with me looking up at her. She waited while my eyes moved from hers to her panties.

"Do you like me standing up here?" she uttered sweetly. "Naughty old man!"

I grinned. "Can't decide which pair I like better."

"These ones have more of a satin feel. The other ones are cotton."

"Yeah, those ones are pretty with the lace. I think the other ones show the shape of your pussy better for us."

Justine smiled. "Well, the other guys like it when I wear the cotton ones swimming, so maybe you should come with us sometime. You can look at me like that when they're nearly see-through and clinging to me," she added teasingly. "Jasper and Steven have been looking!"

Steven walked in with two fish for dinner that night.

"Don't you, Steven! You like it when I wear my cotton panties swimming?" Justine called to him.

"Yep," Steven replied shortly. He eyed me. "You'd look good in a potato sack, Justine. You always look hot."

## Steven

I dumped the fish in the sink for Thomas to finish cleaning. I'd taken on the fishing duties and found a few good spots along the inlet. I'd also seen chickens that must have been turned loose by someone, and I'd caught two of them so far, which made for a good change of food for everyone on those nights.

I was pretty much over withdrawals from missing my computer games and internet. I was a bit of a loner at home where I lived in a small blacked out bedroom. I'd done it tough for the first few weeks but had to get over that if I was going to be stuck here on the island probably for months or whatever. I'd gotten into the outdoor existence, feeling kind of savage and primal. I was turning brown and growing some serious stubble on my chin – loving Justine's hair trimming and getting her to fashion a goatee.

I hadn't come to terms with my place exactly, though – with my relationship to Justine, and with the fact that she was my cousin's wife. I fucking loved the way she was dressing and that. She was the first girl I'd really noticed when I was only 12 and she started coming over with Paul. She was seventeen and used to wear a little white bikini to swim in the pool. I'd started checking her out all the time back then and never really stopped watching her every chance I got since. I always made sure to visit regularly when she and Paul moved in together. They lived on my way home from school, and I used to call in all the time and Justine would give me a drink or a piece of cake or whatever she had baked.

I often lay awake at night wondering if I loved her. I didn't really know what love was, but I had really intense feelings for her that felt like they might be love. And those feelings were worse here on the island, being here with her and living in the same small cabin.

I hadn't worked out what to do or how to feel about the other two men here, though. That next day we had decided to go swimming again, and I was sitting on the bank watching them in the water.

Justine was squealing and laughing and Jasper was playing with her. He always tickled her, and right then he was doing it under the water, probably grabbing her legs, I imagined, because I knew she was really ticklish there.

She finally got away, and Jasper swam over to the waterfall while she came ashore. Thomas was there beside me. He hadn't been in for a swim but had come along that day. Justine waded from the water wringing her hair to one side. She stood in front of us smiling at Thomas. He was looking her over. The blue singlet I had given her was like it was painted on her tits, and her nipples were hard and poking at it. Her panties were as if painted on with a thin water-colour. Her skin was visible through them. We could see her tiny bush and the wet fabric was clinging to her pussy and defining it perfectly. There were two smooth round pillows with a slit between them where your dick goes.

"That looks really beautiful, love," Thomas said to her. "We can see everything so clearly."

She bit down on her lip, fiddling with the waist band of her panties, tugging them up tighter. She took a towel I handed her and dabbed at her face and the ends of her hair, keeping the towel to one side while Thomas stared at her down below.

"They asked me to wear these ones all the time for swimming, didn't you, Steven?"

I nodded to her, glancing up from staring at her panties too.

She dabbed herself dry all over then sat down on the towel with her thighs swayed modestly together. She folded her singlet up over her belly, though. "I'm so glad you men found those other razors for me. I wouldn't like you to see me like this if I was all hairy."

Justine had her back to the water, facing us both. She straightened her legs and Thomas's eyes lowered to her. She watched his face, glancing at me and checking that I was also watching old Thomas checking out her pussy real close and serious now.

"I can see it perfectly, love." His voice was low and kind of gravely. "I can see your little pussy completely through them. I can see each cute little hair and I can see your slit. It's so smooth."

Justine blushed even deeper. She was resting back on her hands, and she bent one leg back up and swayed it across the other. "I don't mind if you look, though," she said and she swayed her leg the other way and opened her thighs. "Jasper's even been trying to touch me sometimes. He says it's been so long here already and he misses women... like, being able to touch and have them touch him."

Thomas swallowed. "Well if you young folks were to um – play around a little – it would be only natural, love."

"No it wouldn't!" I complained. "He shouldn't be touching you at all."

"And I wouldn't let just him!" Justine said to me. "That wouldn't be fair to you, Thomas, or you, Steven. I think we're all as stranded here as each other, and no one should have more of anything than the other."

"Oh! So, we're allowed to tickle you too?" I asked. I liked that idea.

Justine giggled. "Well, I'm not asking for it. If you try it, I'll squeal, but you won't be in trouble for it. I don't think Paul minds too much… Actually, you should do it in front of him if you're going to. That way he's being included in the teasing and fun."

"Speaking of you and Paul, love, I nearly walked in on you yesterday afternoon. We need to find a way to give you more privacy."

"Oh no! I'm sorry, Thomas. We thought you were off somewhere with Jasper. Oh, that's terrible that you couldn't come in. I'm so embarrassed."

"No don't be, love." Thomas chuckled. "If I were your young husband."

"I know, but that's the thing. It's not fair on you other men if we do that. We've been trying to be discrete about it. It's just that being here has um… Well, it's solved a little problem we were having."

"What problem?" I asked, wondering what she was talking about. Although I couldn't stop looking at her pussy. She still had her legs open and I could see it so easily through her wet panties.

"Never mind, just a temporary thing." Justine said about my question, and I looked up and saw her blushing again. "But we won't be doing it anymore, now that we've intruded like that."

"Intruded? Love, I'm the one who almost intruded!"

"No. It isn't fair," Justine declared. "That's why Paul and I don't sleep together. No, you men have to do it for yourself, so, so can we!"

Thomas laughed. "It's damn hard finding a chance for that, isn't it, Steven?"

I blushed myself. "Are you guys talking about what I think you're talking about?"

"Don't try and tell us you don't do it, Steven." Justine pushed me with her foot. "Everyone does it, you know?"

"Yeah, but not everyone talks about it," I said, smiling even though they were hacking on me now.

Also I was getting a boner and I was just staring at Justine's pussy again. She stopped giggling and was quiet for a minute. She was still leaning back on her hands and had her legs bent up. Thomas leant down a bit and was looking real close at her pussy again too. I looked up and she just looked right back at me. Then I leant in next to Thomas and she opened her legs wider.

"Oh love," old Thomas kind of groaned.

"Mmm... but I like you looking," Justine said, and she closed her legs then swung them open again, and my dick was way hard and poking straight up, so I got up and ran and dived into the water.

## Justine

Thomas and I returned to the cabin where Paul was working in his garden. He had found packets of seeds and had shoots up for potentially fresh salad in a month or two. He came inside. I was in my room with the partition drawn back. I looked past where Thomas had stopped, still chatting with me, to where Paul leant in the doorway.

I was wearing a towel around my waist. I remained facing the men while I removed my panties from beneath it. I loosened the towel and tugged it up to my chest, and I pulled my wet singlet from the top of it and over my head.

Paul rolled his eyes. I smiled at him. Thomas had shut up kind of suddenly. I walked past him and to the wash tub where I placed my wet clothes in the water and rubbed a bit of soap.

Paul sat on the couch with his foot up. He started reading one of my books. Thomas brought over some sheets for washing and placed them on the bench. He casually clutched my waist, kneading firmly and tickling me. I squealed and held my towel. He dug his fingers into my ribs, making me shriek with laughter. I clamped my arms tight to my sides, but his big bony hands were strong. I looked to Paul. He was watching, his head raised to see what was happening.

It was so exciting to be looked at in front of my husband, even more so to be touched.

I held Paul's gaze while the older man continued tickling me. His fingers worked their way in under my arms, and with his thumbs kneading my sides, he felt my breasts, quite deliberately, I thought. He kept hold of my left breast and clutched the back of my neck with his other hand. "Ticklish there too?"

I giggled. "No, not there! Meany!" I still had my arm clamped to my side but not so firmly as to stop him from moving the hand beneath there.

He traced fingertips softly across my upper back. "What about there?" he asked, and at the same time, squeezed my breast very deliberately.

I squirmed a little, mostly to turn further from Paul's line of sight. He couldn't have seen me being felt up, as Thomas's hand was beneath one of the folds of the towel. "Yes, a little bit there," I answered as he traced back and forth across my back. He thumbed over my nipple. I could feel his erection pressing against my hip.

Paul came over to the kitchen and poured a glass of water. Thomas extracted his hand from beneath my arm. I fixed the towel from having loosened. Thomas began massaging my shoulders. "Mmm that's better," I cooed, again meeting my husband's gaze.

"Is that nice, love? Do you want more?"

"Ooh yes please?"

"She has lovely slender shoulders," Thomas said to Paul.

He nodded. "And her neck. I love her neck," Paul said, leaning on the sink and just watching.

I was facing him directly. As Thomas massaged, I allowed the top of the towel to loosen away from my breasts, holding the droopy garment with my arms again pressed to my sides. It gradually gaped enough to reveal my nipples. Paul was staring. Thomas was looking down over my shoulder as he continued kneading me firmly and making my breasts rise and fall.

Thomas worked down lower, either side of my spine and then back up to my neck. I allowed my head to rock forward, relaxing into the wonderful sensations as I also allowed the towel to lower to my waist.

I opened my eyes to check on my husband, still watching. The older man was using his thumbs to massage, and his fingers were pressing into my sides, beneath my arms again. I lifted my arms out of his way and let him feel into the sides of my breasts.

I wanted him to feel me properly. My nipples were aching for attention.

"This is so nice," I said, smiling back over my shoulder.

"I used to do massage when I was your age. I worked at a resort for a few years."

"So, you were a professional masseuse?" Paul asked.

"Yeah, when I was young and fit." Thomas kneaded my upper arms, pulling them back and looking down at my boobs. He worked back to my shoulders as I sat down on a stool, then he rubbed down my chest, his thumbs pressing between my breasts and his fingers flaying over them and touching my tight little nipples. He did that again, smoothing from my shoulders all the way down to my stomach, and he squeezed and lifted my breasts more deliberately that time. "But like this is more of a sensual rather than therapeutic massage." Thomas swept his big bony hands down once more and just held my breasts that time, feeling them and thumbing my nipples.

I closed my eyes and enjoyed the stimulation. The way the older man was tweaking my nipples was sending bolts of pleasure straight to my pussy. The feel of his big hands holding and playing with my breasts had me pressing my chest forward for more. He returned to my shoulders for a moment then swept down to squeeze my tits again. I caught my breath and met Paul's eyes that time.

I thrust my chest forward while the older man continued to feel me up. "Mmm that's nice. I think I like getting massaged," I said and looked up at Thomas.

He was glaring down at what he was doing. He had ended the pretence and was just enjoying himself playing with my nipples now. He left them erect and tingling and just looked at me. I kept my tits thrust forward for him. I looked down at them then back up, inviting him to enjoy.

Paul took my hand and pulled me to my feet and against his chest. He kissed me. I moaned into his mouth, still clutching the towel at my waist and with my upper-body bare.

"I think I should leave you young folks to it," Thomas offered, chuckling.

"Good idea. Thanks man," Paul replied.

I was horrified. I broke off my husband's attempt at another kiss. "No! Wait!"

"Yes, it's fine, love. You need your privacy. I'll head back to the pond and make sure the guys don't come back for an hour or so, okay?"

"But no. It's not –" My plea failed to stop the older man from leaving the cabin. My husband pulled me close and tried to kiss me again. He groped my breast but I peeled his hand off it and covered myself with the towel. "No Paul. This isn't right. It's not fair!"

"What's not fair? It's cool, sweetheart. Thomas obviously remembers what it's like to be young."

I checked out the door. Thomas disappeared along the trail. I brushed at Paul's clutching hands again. "No way, Paul. It's not fair... us doing this and him missing out. That's just cruel when there are no women here for the other men. It's not right for us to be taking over the place and making them hide while we have sex."

"Well what are we supposed to do? It's not our fault we got stranded together."

"NOTHING is what we're supposed to do." I folded my arms resolutely. "We'll just have to wait until we get home. Like they have to!"

"Wait? You mean, to have sex?"

"Yes! It won't kill us. You can still do it for yourself, as can I."

"Shit! Seriously? But my dick's finally working again."

I giggled a little. "Well, we've done it a few times now, and that will have to do. I feel terrible. It's just not fair to the others. Not unless you want to share!"

"You mean, share you with them?" Paul asked almost mildly.

I glared. "I wasn't serious!" I saw Paul blush a little. "Oh my god, you meant that."

"No I didn't."

"You did so! I know you, Paul. Have you thought about it before?"

He blushed a bit deeper. "Yeah sort of. I'm not a total arsehole, you know? I feel sorry for the guys being stranded here without women too."

"Oh my god." I pressed close, asking as sweetly as I could, "So, what were you thinking, exactly?"

"Nothing. Just what we said a minute ago… about um – you know – sharing."

"Sharing *me*?" I took a soft kiss, cuddling to my husband's chest. "Would you really do that?"

"No, not really. And I wouldn't expect you would agree to something like that either, baby. I wouldn't offend you by suggesting it."

I fiddled with chest hair. "I don't find the idea offensive. Scary, I guess, but not unpleasant."

"No? Not even with old Thomas?" Paul grinned teasingly.

I blushed that time. "He's only in his 50s. He's only parent old, not grandparent."

Paul chuckled. He sat and I sat on his knee. "It's just with the way you've been flashing them, baby. It's kind of not that big a next step to think about. It would probably be different actually doing it."

"I know. It was interesting with the way Thomas was touching me just now, and Jasper has been getting more handsy with his tickling lately."

"Yeah, I noticed that. Thomas was cool, though. That was hot watching him massage you. I started getting a boner! The idea of him and Steven doesn't worry me. It's just Jasper. If he wasn't here, I'd probably say let's go for it."

*Whoa, hang on a minute. What was this?*

I sought my, suddenly quite intriguing, husband's eyes. "What's wrong with Jasper? He's been really nice since we've been here."

"I know. It's not that. He's been great. We've always gotten on, anyway. It's just that he's different to me... not like the other two."

"Oh. How's that?"

"Well, he's kind of direct competition, if that makes any sense. Thomas is the wrong generation, and Steven's just a kid. But Jasper!"

"Oh I see." I took another kiss. "He's another man. Another potential mate for me?"

"Exactly!"

"Hmm, that's sexy," I whispered into another kiss. "It turns me on thinking about that."

"Yeah?"

"Uh huh. Why don't you check and see?" I tugged at Paul's arm, guiding his hand beneath the front of my towel, parting my legs enough that he could feel where I knew I was dripping.

"Shit you're soaked, sweetheart."

"Uh huh. I need your dick."

"Yeah? But what about..?"

"I know what I said, but I need it." I straddled Paul's thighs. He freed his erection and I got on it. "Mmm that's better."

I clung to my husband as I squirmed on his erection. He cuddled me tight and took longer to cum than I did. My orgasm was still clenching my belly when he tensed up and cried out, ejaculating so hard I felt it spurting inside.

"Wow, you really are cured, Paul. I can't believe how hard you're staying now."

"I know. It's so great to be back to normal."

"No, this is better than normal. You feel stronger than I can remember. You came so hard that time."

"I think it's because of all this teasing. Like, just before when you were swimming with the others and I was here wondering what was going on. That shit gets me on edge really bad."

I stripped my sweaty singlet and pulled on a tunic. "But you know I wouldn't let anything happen behind your back. Not like someone we know!"

"Aaah SHIT. Not that again!"

I giggled. "I'm not going on about it. I'm just teasing this time."

"Oh. That's okay, then? It was, like, three years ago now."

"I know. And I forgave you two years ago." I cuddled my husband again. "But you were very bad once, and that girl was a potential mate for you, wasn't she? She was the same age as me."

"Yeah, but I was drunk. I didn't see her like that, sweetheart. It just happened."

"Yeah, but I'm just saying – about you being worried about Jasper being the competition – that when you did it, it was with someone just like that to me. MY competition."

Paul frowned. "Aw yeah, I get it now. I'm still really sorry about that, baby."

"I know you are. Really, I'm over it." I took a kiss and smiled into it. "But you having to worry about Jasper is fair punishment if you ask me."

"Yeah, whatever. I suppose that's true." Paul sat at the table. I sat too. He looked up with another ponderous frown. "So, what about what we were talking about just before… are you seriously thinking about it?"

"I don't know. I never thought about it before. I just said it as a joke. Although I still think we shouldn't do this together while they can't."

"Yeah I get that. It must be uncomfortable for them wondering if they're going to walk in on us."

"Exactly! But you weren't joking, were you Paul? You would really consider letting them have sex with me, wouldn't you?"

Paul took a moment to respond, rubbing at his fingers. He shrugged. "Yeah... aah, I would, I guess. Definitely with Thomas and Steven, and umm, I guess I could swallow my pride with Jasper if I had to. But there's no way I'd even imagine anything like this at home. It's just that we're stranded here, and everything feels different. There's a freaky native feel to everything. It's like the rules are all different or something."

"Yes, I feel that too," I concurred quickly. "I feel so alive and vibrant. I don't want to not have sex. It's on my mind all the time just looking at you men getting around half naked too. I mean, Steven has a nice body. So does Jasper. And even Thomas is kind of sexy looking. He's in good shape for an older man, and I love his hands. They're so strong."

"Okay. So, let's say we decided to do something like this. What about the fact that there are, like, four men and just you? I mean, it's better than the other way around.

There's no way one man could keep up with four women." Paul chuckled. "I guess he could die trying haha."

I giggled too. "Hmm, I suppose. But I don't know about taking care of so many men in that way. I don't think I'd like it with more than one at a time. And not every five minutes either. I guess I could probably enjoy it as often as once each per day with four men. Especially if sometimes it would just be him getting off, which I'm sure it would be. When I'm tired from doing it so often."

Paul rubbed a spot on the table. "Hmm, three other guys getting off in my wife, huh? That's about what it would be," he pondered, still looking a bit apprehensive, and quite excited too, I sensed

"Well, it certainly wouldn't be emotional or romantic in any way," I said. I wanted to dispel any such idea right away.

"No of course not, baby. We're just talking about a sexual release."

I blushed at the simple idea. "Uh huh. Relieving their tension in the only female on the island. Which could just be in my mouth sometimes, I suppose."

Oh I loved that idea too. Of taking other men in my mouth again, since getting married and being restricted to just the one. It wasn't the taste of course, but I loved the feel of a man in my mouth. Holding me by the hair and making me do it. Filling my mouth with his hot gooey semen.

Paul looked up, his eyes intense. "Yeah, I hadn't thought of that. I guess it would be practical to just do oral sometimes."

"Uh huh. It would be easier for me to stroke and suck them off sometimes, and I think they'd enjoy it just as much, don't you? I mean, if I always went all the way and let them watch me swallow their cum, of course."

Paul nodded, his face flushing red. "Yeah, you'd have to swallow for them. They'd want that for sure."

I smiled through a blush. "Me too, I think."

I would definitely want to swallow for them. I soo love it when a man cums in my mouth and I've always swallowed.

"But I'm still not sure we should do any of this, sweetheart. I think we need to think about it. To be sure we won't regret it later, when we get home."

"I know, Paul. I agree, we need to really think about it first." I got up and cuddled behind my husband to whisper into his ear. "But I will actually do it. I'll let them all have me if that's what we decide."

Paul squeezed my arms. "Okay baby. I'll let them all have you too – if that's what we decide!"

I was walking to the kitchen when Paul called out one last thing.

He chuckled. "As long as Jasper doesn't go first!"

# Paul

I was sitting on the veranda when the other three men returned from swimming. They went inside, but Jasper came back out with a kitchen chair and the hair-trimming cloth for his shoulders. He got set up, and my wife brought her comb and scissors.

She trimmed the back and top while standing behind then moved around to do the sides and his beard. Her tunic had just the one tie, around her waist. It was open above and below. Her hips were bare, the skirt of the garment opening to reveal her pubic hair sometimes. It did so one time when she was stepping across one of Jasper's knees. She had pressed against his arm, and her skirt gathered aside and revealed her fully down below.

Jasper had a look at her pussy. He tilted his head to see. She looked down too and noticed what had happened. A strand of cotton from the frayed edge of the fabric had caught on a button on Jasper's sleeve. He lifted his arm, pulling her skirt up and to the side. She fiddled with the tangled thread while he grinned and examined her.

He winked over at me. "Nice eh?"

I held his gaze for a few seconds before lowering my eyes and looking away, accepting that he was in charge here and could enjoy playing with my wife and looking at her. Possibly even more than that.

The idea of him fucking her seemed only natural in this situation. Yes she was married to me, but Jasper was the alpha male among us here stranded on this island and Justine was the only female.

I looked over at him again but he had dismissed me, it seemed. He obviously felt his dominance and wasn't worried what I thought.

Justine snipped the thread to release it. She brushed her skirt down, blushing as she glanced at me as well. "You did that on purpose, didn't you?" she accused Jasper with a mock glare.

He just smiled up at her as she resumed trimming his beard. He touched her legs, clutching just above her knees.

"Don't! I might snip you if you do it."

He just kept smiling and only softly gripped her. He caressed upward a little and squeezed gently again. Justine combed his hair, checking her work. He felt up higher, gathering the bottom of her skirt and squeezing again. She turned her head and swallowed, her eyes closing and her chest lifting as she drew a breath. He stroked softly upward, gathering her skirt and lifting it with his thumbs. His fingers were travelling up the front of her thighs and touched her groin, either side of her little landing strip. He tucked her skirt into her waist band, keeping her revealed.

"That time was on purpose," he said.

Justine glanced at me again. She stood combing her own hair while Jasper continued stroking her legs and looking at her pussy. He was running his fingertips up and down the outer of her thighs with his thumbs caressing the front.

I could feel the guy's eyes upon my face as he glanced a few times. He was blatantly examining my wife now, imagining how she was going to be to fuck, no doubt. It was inevitable that he would be taking her to her room before much longer, pulling the curtain closed and screwing her while I waited in the main room or outside here. I was twisted between hating the idea and wanting it to happen.

I met another of his glances and held his stare for a few long seconds. I felt my face draining of colour but my wife was looking at me too and I glanced and flushed hot again while looking from her eyes to his. Jasper smirked the tiniest bit at me then winked at my wife. In that instant, we all knew who the dominant male was.

It was only a matter of time until he would be sticking his cock up my wife's cunt. He knew it, she needed it, and I couldn't understand why I wanted it. I just hoped he wasn't going to be huge and way bigger than me.

He had resumed examining what he was going to be claiming. On one upward caress of her bare legs, he reached further with his thumbs and touched her inner thighs. She squirmed away before he touched her opening, and she brushed her skirt down. Then Jasper grabbed her and tickled her ribs.

Justine squealed and laughed. He pulled her to him. She wriggled around and he held her from behind. She was squirming and pushing at his arm. I saw he had one arm inside her tunic and that he was groping her bare tit with that hand while tickling her with the other. He reached down and clutched her legs, making her bend forward and virtually sit on his lap.

He relented while she caught her breath. "Don't!" she said, glaring back at him as he threatened to grip her thigh again. She was still giggling and trying to hold that wrist away.

I could see his other hand still feeling her tit. He was massaging it slowly and playing with the nipple. He clutched her thigh gently.

"But don't squeeze," Justine pled. She held his other arm softly as he continued feeling her up. He clutched higher up her thigh and she gripped his wrist in readiness to push him away. He then felt up between her thighs as he suddenly tickled her ribs.

Justine squealed and squirmed. He held her tight and continued tickling her ribs while forcing his other hand up between her legs, which she had firmly pressed together. She shrieked and wriggled and her legs finally opened for him to grope her pussy, but she jumped up off his lap and broke away. "Bad, bad, Jasper!" she scolded, hiding behind me.

Jasper laughed, and she did too. I met the other man's gaze and wink. "Damn she's hot, buddy," he said.

"Yes she is," I agreed, cuddling Justine to my side.

Thomas called that dinner was ready. Justine brushed at the hair all over her tunic, complaining about it as we went inside. She changed behind her partition and came out wearing her frock.

After the meal, I helped Justine with the dishes, as I always did now. We just spoke with our eyes and knowing glances. Her frock had spaghetti string shoulder straps but was also a gathered elastic bodice.

Justine slipped her arms through the strings and left them hanging down. "In case I get tickled again," she whispered to me.

"Do you have anything on underneath?" I whispered back.

She shook her head, biting a grin. "Jasper touched my pussy before, did you see?"

"Yeah. I thought he did."

"I think he might grab me again if I walk too close. I think next time he gets a chance he might finger me."

I nodded, swallowed hard. "Okay... I guess I want it to happen too now," I admitted. "Where did Steven and

Thomas go?" I had seen them leave. Jasper was sitting at the table reading.

"They said something about checking a fishing net they made."

"Okay. Well, I'm going to sit out on the veranda for a while. Are you okay to finish clearing the table?"

Justine blushed a little. "You mean with him sitting there and no one else around?"

I nodded. "I'll be just outside."

"Okay," Justine uttered.

My heart was thumping, my entire body alight with trepidation and excitement. I left my wife and nodded to Jasper as he glanced up. I went out and sat watching the clouds and the moon but listening intently for any sounds from inside the cabin. Moments passed before I heard voices. Then Justine giggled and shrieked.

I looked through the window to see Jasper holding her from behind again. She was pushing a hand away from her leg. She was smiling and pressing back against him, her face red, her eyes alight. He felt one tit then the other. She kept hold of his other wrist and reached back to hold his hip with her free hand. He felt up under her frock. She kept hold of his wrist and had her thighs pressed together. Her eyes closed as he obviously touched her cunt. She gripped the back of his head, her legs giving way as he forced his hand between them.

It looked like he was fingering her. His hand was concealed beneath her frock, but his forearm was flexing and I was sure he had fingers inside her. My gut was twisted tight and my heart was in my throat. I wanted him to drag her to the bed and fuck her right then, but Thomas and Steven were coming up from the beach, so I went to the door and noisily shifted a chair to announce I was coming in.

Justine was fixing the top of her frock. Jasper was resting back in his chair, smiling. At a glance, I could see his fingers were wet.

"He grabbed me again," Justine reported, poking her tongue out at Jasper and having to jump as he lunged for her.

Steven and Thomas came in carrying a couple of crabs in a net basket. They washed up, and cards were dealt.

Justine read while us men played. She went to bed early with her partition half drawn and her bed in the moonlight from her window. We could see her as she pulled on panties and removed her frock. She lay back with her sheet up to her waist and her tits bare. Everyone was looking at her.

"It's not too bright out here, love?" Thomas asked.

"No it's fine. I don't mind the candlelight."

"Yeah, they look nice in the candlelight." Jasper chuckled. "Nice nips."

She patted the sheet down either side of her body, her chest lifting, her nipples erect and casting shadows of their own. "Thank you, Jasper. I'm glad you like them," she said sweetly and yawned.

"I like them too!" Steven said.

Justine giggled, making her tits shudder. "Thank you, Steven."

"Me too," I said, and everyone laughed.

"Lucky arsehole," Jasper scoffed. "At least you've got your woman here with you."

"Yeah I know. We were talking about that earlier, weren't we, sweetheart?"

Justine sat up. "It must be hard for you other men," she offered sincerely.

Thomas moved his chair back to include Justine more directly.

Jasper stood and came around the table. "It could be worse. Like, with no women at all." He sat on the edge of the table, facing Justine.

Steven was nodding to everyone. "Yeah, it's much better with Justine here." He was peering around the edge of the partition.

Jasper was standing there. He pulled it back further, casting more light. Justine looked down at her bare breasts then up at everyone. She was resting back on her hands with them thrust forward. Her nipples were still erect.

She looked up from them. "Are you men sure this doesn't make it harder for you?" she asked sweetly.

"Only in a good way," Thomas answered first.

"Definitely not," Jasper declared forthrightly.

Justine nodded and looked to me. I held her gaze, shrugging an *okay*. We each knew what the other was thinking, though I wasn't sure how far my wife had progressed with what we had spoken about earlier. I understood Justine was about to invite the others into the issue. She was asking if she should say something or whether I wanted to. I mouthed the words *you can*.

"Well, what if we did a little bit more?" she started, peering from Thomas to Jasper. "Paul and I were talking about it and wondering if we should put aside the fact that we're married, in the real world, and do what we can to share everything here."

Jasper's jaw had sagged. Thomas spoke. "To share — everything?"

Justine's blush was noticeable even in the candlelight. "Uh huh. To share me, as the only female here."

Thomas's jaw was sagging now. Steven's eyes were wide as he looked from Justine to us other men. I swallowed hard. Jasper was nodding, a tiny grin curving his lips.

"But I don't mean fully," Justine went on. She had only paused for a split second, but time had slowed for me. "I don't mean having full sex with me. Just, um… well, a little bit less than full but more than you've already been having. Which no one said you could, by the way," she scolded.

Jasper chuckled. "We've been trying to behave."

"Hmm, and you're the worst!" She giggled. "I think if we do anything more, then you should have to go last."

Thomas sat on the end of the cot. Justine had sat forward, hugging her knees.

"What do you mean by *a little more*, love? You shouldn't do anything you're uncomfortable with… or you, Paul."

I met the gazes of the other three men. "Well, we haven't decided anything yet. We're just talking about it and thinking it through at the moment. It feels kind of weird, but this whole situation is freaky."

"Got that right, buddy," Jasper agreed. "You wouldn't read about this shit, but I reckon you and Justine are handling it well. It's great that you're both so open and considerate. I'd like to think I'd be the same if I were here with my woman and you three ugly mugs."

"Oh yeah, and which woman would that be?" Thomas tossed at the younger man.

"You mean, who would I prefer to be stranded on a desert island with?" Jasper frowned in thought. He shook his head. "Nah forget that idea. I'll stick with Justine, thanks."

Everyone laughed. I edged onto the cot beside my wife, taking her hands within one of mine and squeezing. She rocked her head onto my shoulder. I kissed her softly and rested back, cuddling her to my chest. Her tits were then exposed to the other men again.

Thomas looked up from them. "So, what did you mean by *a little bit more*, love?"

"Um. I was thinking of oral. That's something I really enjoy, so if you men wanted it from me… well, I don't see the harm."

"All of us?" Steven blurted.

Justine nodded, biting her lip. "But not every five minutes. With four of you and only one of me!"

Thomas cleared his throat. "That would be amazing, love."

Justine smiled through a deepening blush. "I'll try and make it nice for you... to suck you really nice while you watch me."

"Oh love, that would be a sight to see."

"Best offer I've ever heard of," Jasper said. "What the hell, man?" he tossed at me. "How did you score a wife like this? What's your secret, dude?"

"He's a good kisser," Justine said, peering up at me.

"So, it's for everyone?" Steven asked. "Even..?" He pointed at himself.

"Yes, even for you," Justine answered sweetly. "Of course for you too, Steven. You're stuck here the same as all of us."

"So, when?" Jasper asked, grinning.

Justine blushed again. "Um. What about starting tomorrow? I need to psych myself up." She giggled. "And don't forget, you're last."

"Aw shit. Seriously?"

"Yes, and it won't be one after the other either. I'll need a rest in between."

"A rest between drinks, eh?" Jasper quipped, and Justine tossed a hairbrush at him.

"Actually – yes – exactly that. I don't know how the porno girls do it. It tastes too strong for me to even imagine swallowing from one of you and then another mouthful straight after. I mean, I won't mind if you each give me a nice big mouthful when it's your turn."

"Oh, man, I've got a boner now," Jasper groaned, moving it to the side in his shorts and tapping it with the hair brush.

"I don't think I'll be rolling out of bed tonight either," Thomas said, chuckling. He was hiding his erection.

"Well, I'll fix them for you in the morning, okay? The first time right away and after that we'll see."

"And what about you, love?"

Justine looked up at me. "I think I'll be fine. My husband can take care of me."

Jasper approached beside the bed. He nodded to me. "This is going to be good, man. Make things a whole lot easier here, eh," he said and felt Justine's tits.

"Uh huh huh," she moaned but bit down on that and just thrust her chest forward. She had her arm back and out of the way. I just held her head and kissed her hair.

Jasper was feeling her with one hand and squeezing his cock in his pants with the other. "So you like to swallow, baby? My nuts are feeling pretty fucking full already."

"Yes, I like to swallow," Justine said, looking around at the other two men as well. She grimaced. "I'll enjoy swallowing as much as you can all produce each day as long as I get a rest between."

Jasper stroked down over her belly, collecting the bed sheet and uncovering her panties. He hooked them with a finger and her belly shuddered as he stretched them down and revealed her cunt. "So she'll suck our cocks and swallow our loads, and you'll look after her yourself eh, man?" Jasper directed at me. "You'll look after this, yeah?" he said and turned his hand, still with Justine's panties stretched over the back of it, and he inserted fingers up her, making her moan and grip my arm tight.

"Oh that's nice," Thomas groaned appreciably.

Jasper grinned at him. "She was wet earlier too. Got the same problem as us by the looks."

"Mmm how could I not have?" my wife complained and gripped Jasper's wrist, holding it as he continued, his fingers squelching in her.

Thomas took over stretching the front of her panties down. Steven was gawking over his shoulder. Justine had her legs down straight and her thighs squeezed together. Jasper smirked. "We get to have a little play and a poke while she's sucking our cock, yeah?" he directed at me. "You like being fingered while you suck, don't you baby?"

"Mmm yes, but not like this with everyone watching," Justine scolded.

Jasper chuckled. He was only playing in her. I could see he wasn't touching her clit. He extracted his fingers and joined Thomas keeping the front of her panties stretched down while the three of them tilted in for a close examination. Justine lay still with her fingers twirling her hair as she watched their faces.

"You want us to take these off, baby? They're going to get wet if we pull them up now," Jasper said.

My wife expelled a breath, her tits shuddering in the candlelight. "Okay but not you dirty men. Let Steven take them off me," she answered and Thomas and Jasper laughed and urged the young guy forward.

"Aw shit," he cried worriedly but rubbed his hands together and looked to the task before him.

"It's okay, I don't mind now that we've talked like this," Justine encouraged him. "I don't mind you doing it, Steven. Just not him!" she scolded Jasper and made everyone laugh again.

"Aw shit, aw shit," my young cousin whimpered and took hold of my wife's panties, which the other men had left partially pulled down anyway, her pussy bare and glistening wet in the dim light.

Justine lifted her bottom and Steven pulled her panties down properly, all the way to her ankles and removed them. Jasper cheering and old Thomas slapping the boy's back as he smiled proudly around at us all and held up his prize, twirling it on a finger and getting scolded by my indignant wife and told not to let Jasper influence him if he wanted to be allowed any favours in future.

I was settled into this now. My wife nude there lying on a bed with three other men enjoying looking at her. Her thighs still resolutely pressed together but her opening obviously wet and her nipples constantly at attention until she decided the show was over after ten minutes and sent us all away, pulling up the sheet and rolling over to go to sleep.

## Thomas

I woke at dawn. I got up quietly and peeped in on Justine. She had her sheet pulled up, covering her well. Paul opened his eyes. He had the spot just beyond the partition, of course.

I nodded. "I'll put on some coffee."

"Okay, thanks."

Paul joined me on the veranda to watch the sun rise. I decided not to say anything about Justine. I didn't want to risk the young couple changing their minds. I loved Justine. She was such a sweet girl. Her father, however, in spite of being a good friend, had always looked down on me a little. The man was full of himself and arrogant toward everyone. There were two good reasons I was so looking forward to being with Justine, her beauty and her father's superiority complex. I had two completely different reasons to want the same thing.

"I'm going for a walk on the beach, Paul. I'll make breakfast when I get back."

"Sure Thomas, or I could cook this morning if you want?"

I agreed and left the younger man. I strolled for an hour tossing sticks into the waves and wondering about home. Whether I would ever get back, whether I even cared as long as the supplies held out.

It was a warm summer morning. The sun was high over the ocean by the time I returned to the cabin. Paul and Steven were sitting on the steps.

"You can't go in," Steven said. "Jasper's in there with Justine."

"Oh! Already?"

Paul nodded. "Yeah, he couldn't wait any longer. Justine agreed to start."

"So, you haven't yet, Steven?"

"No. Jasper went first. He's been in there for a while."

All was quiet inside the cabin. I sat on the steps to wait with Steven and Paul. Paul was fiddling with a piece of rope, twisting it anxiously.

The cabin door finally opened, and Jasper walked out fixing the tie in his board shorts. He was grinning and gave me a wink. He sat back in a chair, relaxing with his hands behind his head.

Justine came out a little sheepishly. I could see how red her lips were, her cheeks rosy, her hair ruffled. She sat beside her husband.

"Are you okay, sweetheart?" he asked softly.

She nodded. "I'm fine." She swallowed and opened her mouth. "Salty," she explained.

"Do you want a drink?" Paul asked.

117

"Not yet. I'll get one in a minute."

"It's good, yeah?" Jasper teased.

Justine gulped and opened her mouth again. "I think it's better when men eat lots of sweets or fruit. It's not so strong to taste like this. It's filling my senses, nearly making my eyes water." She giggled. "You big meany!"

Jasper chuckled. "You'll get used to it."

She blushed back at him. "I'll try."

"So, who's next?" Steven asked, looking from Paul to me.

"You can be next, Steven," Justine said sweetly. "But you have to wait a while, okay? I'll say when."

"Okay, you say when. Anytime you say, I'll be ready."

Everyone laughed at the young guy's innocent enthusiasm.

"Is that okay, to wait until later?" Justine asked me.

"That's fine, love. You'd better take care of the young man first."

"I will. Just an hour between so it settles in my stomach." She included Paul as she spoke. His face reddened. She touched his cheek. "It was also quite a lot," she said, glaring across at Jasper.

"Ooh yeah, two balls full, baby," he teased.

She poked her tongue out at him. "Proud of yourself, aren't you?"

He gave her a thumbs up, grinning.

"Well, next time I might not let you hold back so much if you're going to be cheeky. What if I don't let you make them so full?"

"Aw, but that's the fun bit – bring it on slow – fill them up nice and tight – big mouth full."

"Hmm. Well, if you want it like that again next time, you have to behave," Justine scolded.

"Okay. I'll behave."

"Good!"

Justine gulped again, holding her stomach. "Ugh, that's so heavy going down."

"Can I get you some tea?" I asked.

She nodded, blushing a little. "Thanks. I'll come and get some in a minute, but I don't want to wash away the taste yet."

"Fuck yeah," Jasper groaned proudly. "She likes the taste of my ball juice!"

Justine glared defiantly. "I'm not saying I like it in that way. It's just exciting to have it filling my senses like this and for you to obviously enjoy that it is!"

"Yes and to let him enjoy that his semen is coating the inside of your mouth, eh love. That's sexy of you," Thomas encouraged, squeezing Justine's shoulders.

"Uh huh it's definitely coating my mouth… It's one of the reasons I want to wait a while between each of you. So you can have yours coating my teeth and tongue like this for a while too."

"Oh yeah so that's why you didn't swallow right away. Held it in to savour the taste, didn't you baby!"

Justine got up and raked her hair back, pushing Jasper's foot from the rail and making his chair thump down. "Meany!" she scolded, smiling.

He tugged the skirt of her frock, pulling her closer. She held her husband's eyes as she sat back onto Jasper's lap. Her shoulder strings were hanging down. Jasper hooked them both in his fingers, and she lifted her arms through.

He kept tugging until the top of her dress rolled down and almost revealed her nipples. She pressed her arms to her sides. "No!" she uttered. "Not in the daytime, okay? Like that's far enough."

Justine raked her hair back with both arms raised. Jasper covered her tits and massaged them firmly. Her eyes closed for a moment, her chest lifting as she bit down on her lip. "Um. That's enough of that, you!"

He smiled at Steven. "She likes you playing with them while she's doing it, Stevo."

"Doing it?"

"Yeah, you know." Jasper poked his tongue into his cheek and used his fist to simulate a blow job.

Justine punched his arm. She giggled. "You're bad!"

He pushed her off his lap. "And I've got to go."

## Justine

Jasper went to the toilet. Thomas went inside to make tea. I sat back on the veranda rail beside Steven. "Are you okay, Steve?" He looked tense.

"I don't know, you guys, are you sure this is alright?"

"It's fine. We talked about it, didn't we Paul."

"Yeah don't worry, Stevo. It's all cool."

"But Justine's your wife, and she's already sucked off another dude!"

I felt myself blushing. "Well, I've done that for guys before, you know. Before Paul and I met. It's not like it was the first time ever with another man."

"Really? How many?"

"What?" I giggled. "Um. Let me think." I counted off with my fingers. "Six! Now with Paul and Jasper makes eight. But I've only had full sex with three, including Paul."

"Oh. Is that a lot?"

"No!" I cried, pushing the younger guy's shoulder.

"What about you, Steve, how many girls have given you a BJ so far?" Paul asked, grinning up from where he was still sitting on the stairs.

Steven shrugged and shook his head. "None yet."

"Oh really?" I asked smiling and tickling his belly.

"And you haven't been laid yet either?" Paul asked, without any tease in his tone. "That's cool if you haven't. I was older than you the first time I got lucky."

"Yes, it's cute and sweet," I added sincerely. "Maybe you should wait for the right girl? You don't have to do anything right now."

"No, I'd like to do it with you," Steven responded quickly. "It's perfect because we've known each other for ages. It would be nice to try it with you for my first time. Except me and you are cousins, Paul. Are you sure it's alright?"

Paul met my gaze. He nodded, making me blush a little more. "Yeah it's okay, Steve." He still held my eyes. "You can just go with it and enjoy, Stevo. She does it good too. You'll be lucky to find another girl later who gives a nice blowjob like Justine."

I challenged my husband with a mock glare. "That's because I enjoy doing it, Steven. I learned how to make it feel nice for guys back at school. I could tell how much Jasper liked it too!"

I grabbed Steven's belly again. He laughed and held my arms away. He grabbed for my ribs and made me shriek and squirm, but he held on and pulled me close. He was tall and lanky. He wrapped a thin arm around me from behind and I stopped struggling and rested back against him.

We were facing Paul. Steven remained quiet and moved his hand from clutching my side to cup my breast. I swallowed and held a breath as he felt me, squeezing then isolating my nipple. I relaxed my arms, reaching back to hold his hips.

"Is this okay?" he asked, his voice a dry whisper.

I looked to Paul. I nodded. "Yes, it's okay," I told Steven.

"It's better inside her dress. Feel down the front," Paul said, and my face heated instantly.

Steven complied. He wormed his fingers beneath the tight elasticated fabric and squeezed my left breast bare. I let escape a ragged breath, squirming back against his erection. "Um. Steven!" I moaned softly as he moved to my right breast and felt it as well. He groped and squeezed, rolling that nipple between his fingers. His other hand was on my belly. I gripped his wrist and pushed it lower, pressing my thighs together as he instinctively found the slit between my pussy lips. He rubbed me through the skirt of my dress and my panties, which I had worn to discourage Jasper from venturing down there.

"Should we go for a walk, Steven?" I asked back over my shoulder. "Are you ready?"

"I'm ready!"

I took his hand and leaned down to whisper into Paul's ear. "Won't be long, okay?"

Paul nodded and squeezed my other hand as I passed down the steps.

Jasper walked around the corner of the cabin. "Ooh yeah! Go for it, Stevo."

"I am!" Steven called back. "I'm getting it now, Jasper!"

I shook my head, blushing. "Don't listen to him, Steven."

"Why? Jasper's the man," the young guy replied cheekily, and he clutched my ribs, making me squeal. Then he grabbed me around the waist and tickled me some more.

I doubled over laughing and squirming with my arms pinned tight against my sides. He attacked my knees, and as I tried to hold his arms away, he put a hand up the skirt of my frock. I clamped an arm across my belly but he wormed beneath, and I relaxed my arm as, instead of tickling, he felt my tits.

"But Steven!" I complained softly. We had reached the trail to the beach but were still within sight of the cabin. Paul and the other two men were watching, their heads raised. I leaned on a branch of a small tree. I held it with one hand. Where I had my other arm across my body, I gathered the folds of my bunched-up frock and held it there. Steven was kissing my shoulder and still groping my breasts. His other hand was upon my hip, touching the waistband of my panties. They were exposed to the men watching.

"Go Stevo!" Jasper called out.

Steven pressed into my groin more deliberately. He felt around to the front of my panties, rubbing my landing strip then searching lower into my moist heat. I released my frock and felt back to his hip, pulling him against me.

"Not inside, okay? Just through my panties."

"Okay," he breathed into my neck, still kissing me there as he pinched and rolled a nipple and poked into my slit with his long, thin fingers.

I felt his package. He was hard, his dick vertical. "Oh wow! Steven!" It was extremely long… kind of slender, but longer than any I had felt before.

"I know. It's pretty big, huh?"

"It's huge! Oh my god. You'll have to be careful when you get a real girlfriend."

"I know. Thomas told me about that."

"Thomas did?"

"Yeah, because he's like this too, so he says. But my dad isn't, so I must have got it from Mum's side."

I squeezed it. He thrust against my hand. "Um. It's nearly happening," he groaned.

"Okay. Can you walk? Can we go somewhere?" I asked him.

"Um. It's close though, Justine. Sorry!"

"No that's okay. Just there, then." I urged him behind the tree and got on my knees.

"Ooh yeah!" Jasper called out. "Give it to her, Stevo!"

I pulled the front of his shorts and underpants down and quickly took him in my mouth. He grabbed my hair and thrust. I kept a hold on his shaft so he didn't go down my throat. He jiggled and humped my hand and mouth for a minute then held firm, groaning as his cock flexed and pulsed, heavy bursts of semen gushing against the back of my mouth.

I swallowed softly, holding the tapered head of Steven's cock in my mouth, my eyes closed and his hand now at rest upon the back of my head. I felt the underside of the glans with my tongue, teasing the eyelet, which was still dribbling cum with each soft throb. I swallowed again and kissed the tip of his dick. The shaft had softened. I released it from my fist and held it up to kiss my way down to his sac. It was lightly haired, his balls tight within it. I nuzzled them and kissed each one softly. He was watching intently. I smiled up at him.

"I love you now, Justine."

I giggled. "I've actually heard that before while doing this, Steven."

He smiled. "Well, it feels like I do."

"That's good. And I love you too while we're playing like this."

I kissed my way back along his shaft and sucked the head into my mouth. I took him deeper, until he was pressing into my throat. I couldn't go any further, had never been able to do that. I had taken most of his length though, and I slowly bobbed my head back and forth, letting him slide in and out until he became hard again. I used my hand and stroked fast over the swollen head. I kept him wet and jerked him to another climax, capturing the head of his cock in my mouth as he began to ejaculate.

He produced another three or four heavy spurts, and I closed my eyes and moved it around in my mouth, coating my tongue and teeth and drawing it into my senses. I then let the thick, gooey pool seep into my throat and I peered up at the guy as I swallowed his cum. "Mmm you taste so strong Steven." I cupped his balls and held them softly, kissing the reddened dome of his cock again. "Is that better?"

"That was awesome, Justine. That's the best thing ever!"

"Okay well, I'll do that for you from now on, while we're stuck here. You can have my mouth like that and I'll swallow your cum, but not every five minutes. Maybe once each day or something, unless I'm not in the mood for sexy fun. Like at that time of the month."

Steven blushed. "Oh. That time!"

I got up, brushing at my grassy knees. "So, you know about girl stuff, do you?"

"A bit. We had classes at school. Plus, with my sisters. They get cranky, I've noticed."

"Hmm well, so do I. So, you'll know when not to bother me for blowjobs, won't you?"

He chuckled. "Yep. I'll know alright. But how will I know when to ask on usual days?"

"Well, I was thinking about that." I raked my hair and fixed it with a cloth ribbon I had made. "I was thinking it might be best if you men knew what to expect. I mean, it's not very romantic to have it all planned, but it's not about romance, it's about me looking after your needs and keeping your balls all empty and soothed, isn't it," I teased, looking at where the guy was still holding himself.

"Do they feel empty?" I asked more seriously. "I can swallow extra for you this first time if you need me to?"

"Um no that's okay. I've been doing it for myself all the time in the forest thinking about you, so I'm a bit drained right now," he said, blushing.

"Okay good… So anyway, I was thinking if it was Jasper in the morning, you in the afternoon and Thomas after dinner. Or something like that. So that way, you'd know I'm going to do it for you after lunch, and you wouldn't have to be hanging around wondering at any other time. Does that sound silly?"

Steven shook his head emphatically. "Nope. It sounds perfect. There's no question what's happening, and no one can take anyone's turn."

I giggled. "Taking your turn, huh? It sounds naughty when you say it like that."

He shrugged. "But that's what it is."

"Yeah I guess. And you guys will have to let my husband and I go to bed early some nights so we can have our turn."

"Yep. Definitely! Just tell me when to get lost and I will."

"Okay, now I just have to explain all of that to the others somehow."

# Justine

I held my husband's gaze as I walked toward him still sitting on the steps. I wrung my hands in front, trying to read his expression. His lips curved slightly upward. I smiled.

Jasper was leaning on the rail. "How'd you go, Stevo, get a good load off?"

Steven held up two fingers.

"Two loads?" Jasper cried.

"Yep. It was awesome!"

Thomas came out with a cup of tea for me.

"Thank you, Thomas. I need to eat something too. I need something else in my stomach besides all you guys' gooey stuff." I sipped some tea, which felt nice going down. "I was just saying to Steven, I think we should do this after meals from now on. I won't mind if you guys each have a set time for your sexy fun. At least I'd know what was happening, and so would you. Unless that sounds silly?"

"I like that," Thomas replied quickly. "That's clear and simple." He shrugged. "Can I be in the evening? At my age testosterone levels rise toward night-time. I'm not much good in the morning these days."

Jasper grinned. "I'll go first. Love a morning BJ."

I met Steven's smile. He shrugged. "Just like you said." He looked up at the other men. "And we all have to get lost when Justine and Paul wanna do it at night."

Thomas chuckled. Jasper winked at Paul. "Fair enough, buddy."

Paul nodded and gave a shrug. "Yep, sounds fair to me."

I squeezed Paul's arm. I was sitting beside him, cuddling it. "This is going to be great," I said to him. "It's going to be fun."

"What about for you though, love, will you be okay with giving oral so often? There's nothing wrong with a good old hand job, you know?"

I giggled. "I know. Maybe a bit of one, a bit of the other. I won't mind unless it's my time of the month. That should be next week, so I might be unavailable for a few days. I usually get cramps and that. It's pretty yucky."

"We've got plenty of pain killers yet, and there's a hot water bottle."

"Really? That will be great at night."

"Yeah, I found one on top of the pantry, love. Probably some other lady here with the same idea. My Margie used to swear by the old hot water bottle."

"I know. They're brilliant. Thank you, Thomas. You're so considerate."

"Yeah, sucking up," Jasper scoffed. "He knows he's next."

We all laughed. I left the men to go and find food. Thomas sat me down at the table and served me fish soup and his quite yummy dough biscuits for lunch. He had developed a recipe for the biscuits over a number of failed attempts. They were pretty good now.

Paul had gardening to do. Jasper had wood to cut. Steven went fishing for the afternoon.

When I finished my lunch, Thomas cleared away my bowl. "So, I should be ready for our liaison after dinner tonight?" he asked, grinning.

"Uh huh. Do you mind waiting? It will be nicer for me if we wait a few hours. I'm not used to swallowing so much semen in one day."

"That's fine, love. I'm happy to wait. The anticipation is very exciting, and like I said, I perform much better in the evening."

I smiled up at the older man as he approached behind me. He placed his hands upon my shoulders and pressed his thumbs either side of my spine. My head rocked forward. "Mmm that feels so nice."

He began massaging me, working the tension from my shoulders and upper back. My shoulder strings were hanging down. I slipped my arms through as Thomas adjusted the top of my dress, tugging it down a little. He rested me forward over the table and resumed massaging my back, working lower now and kneading the muscles either side of my spine down to the base. My breasts popped out the top of my dress, but I remained bent down with them pressed against the table.

Thomas rubbed up my sides and down as far as my hips. He returned to my neck, and I sat up, lifting the top of my dress to cover myself. "Is that all nice and soothed now, love?"

"It's wonderful. Thank you, Thomas."

"It's much better with oils. You have lovely soft skin though."

I rested back in the chair as he rubbed down my chest. He used only one hand and slipped it down the front of my frock. He felt my left breast, covering it with his hand and kneading it. "There's not really a muscle group here, love. It's more for stimulation."

"Uh huh."

"You have very responsive nipples." He tweaked that one then moved to the other, just kneading the back of my neck with his other hand.

I opened my eyes to see Paul watching from the window. I held his gaze while the older man continued feeling me up. He swept both hands down between my boobs and cupped them, my frock slipping down to my waist. He claimed both of my nipples and pinched them a little harder. "Is that okay, love?"

"Uh huh."

He pinched harder, twisting as well. "And that?"

"Not too hard!"

He relented and resumed massaging my breasts and gently caressing my nipples. He concentrated on one, squeezing my boob and running a fingertip around the areola. He wet his finger and used his saliva to make it slippery and cool. I met Paul's gaze again. He was watching what Thomas was doing. Thomas leaned down and suckled that nipple. I caught my breath and nursed his head. He sucked half my tit into his mouth and lashed the nipple with his tongue. I moaned my pleasure at the tantalising sensation that rocketed down to my pussy.

His hand closed over my thigh. It moved upward and squeezed again. He moved to my other tit and sucked hard then lashed the nipple, swirling his tongue around it and flicking over it. His hand moved again, his long bony fingers kneading and pressing against the edge of my underwear. "Um Thomas!"

"I know, love. Just your little clitty through your panties, okay?" He found my clit and rolled a fingertip around it. It was engorged and needed petting badly.

"Uh huh huh," I moaned raggedly as he pressed more firmly and isolated it.

"You can have a nice little orgasm if you like, love. Clit and nipples. Do you like them like that?"

"Uh huh, I like that," I said, gripping his head and squirming against the teasingly soft ministrations of his fingers down below. I checked on Paul. He was still watching but wouldn't have been able to see what was happening beneath the table. The lashing of the older man's tongue and pressure of his fingers against my clit soon sent me over the edge into orgasm. I disguised it from Paul as best I could, my belly clenching nicely, but Thomas seemed to know enough to ease up when I became too sensitive. Both my nipples and clit were alight with exquisite sensations of pleasure.

Thomas lifted from my breasts, pulling my frock up to cover them. I peered up at him and instinctively parted my lips as he pressed his to them. He kissed me softly, lingering a few seconds and touching my lower lip with his tongue. I bit that lip when he lifted from me. I added a blush and half smile.

Paul cleared his throat from the doorway. I blushed at him too, tugging my frock up a bit straighter.

"Sorry, were you um..?"

"No, not that. Not until after dinner," I said. "I was just getting treated to another nice massage for now."

"Yes, mostly therapeutic, a little bit of sensual," Thomas added, rubbing my shoulders. "She's hard to resist being sensual with, isn't she?"

"Yes, that's true. She's a sensual girl," Paul said.

"Indeed," Thomas went on smoothing down my front once more. He felt my tits again. I reached up to the back of his neck. He slid his hands down my dress and felt me bare. "Very hard to resist," he went on.

"Hmm, but you have to wait until tonight now," I uttered, catching my dress and pulling it back up.

Thomas patted Paul's shoulder on his way out the door. Paul took a seat at the table with me. "Did he just finger you, sweetheart?"

"No, he just rubbed me down there. Just through my panties."

Paul nodded slowly. "So, they've all gone that far now. Have any of them actually fingered you yet?"

"Not yet, other than Jasper a little bit. Are they allowed to?"

My husband took my hand, holding my fingers and stroking with his thumb. He looked up from the table. "I thought you got it exactly right, baby. I like that you drew the line at no 'full sex' and that you've got them organized so that they're not going to be hanging around trying to get onto you every five minutes." Paul grimaced. "It's pretty freaky just watching them with you. It's like a frigging dream or something. Like it's not even real."

"A dream or a nightmare?"

"No a dream! It's hot and it's freaky, but not in a bad way. Except with Jasper a little bit, but I'm getting used to it."

"I know. We couldn't stop him going first, could we?" I uttered. "He's so pushy."

"Yeah it was hard waiting out there that first time when he took you inside. Then it was so quiet, and it took so long before you came back out."

I blushed. "It's because he kept holding back. He kept getting close then making me go slow and letting him build up more. He only came the once, but it was pretty huge. I was starting to get my achy jaw, so it was a relief when he finally came, and I just had to swallow it all for him." I made a mock yucky face to illustrate how I remembered the big mouthful of cum Jasper had fed me. "But Steven was the opposite. He came so fast! Then I let him have another turn to make sure he finished satisfied. I can't believe how much semen I've swallowed so far today. But it's fine. I think I'll be fine doing this each day. I'll just have to use my hand more sometimes and only take them into my mouth when they're ready to cum."

"Or maybe you don't always have to take them in your mouth, baby. There's nothing wrong with just a hand job."

"Yeah, I know." I smiled through my blush... bit my lip. "But I like eating it for them. It's so sexy when they're watching my face while they're blowing. Having my head held and being made to swallow their cum. I know guys love that, but so do I."

Paul nodded. "Yeah I guess." His face reddened too. "And I guess it's fair enough, them touching you. And even if they try and finger you, or like with Thomas sucking your tits before."

"Uh huh and what about when he kissed me?"

"Well, that's hardly anything compared to the rest, baby."

"Do you think? Kissing is very intimate, Paul."

Paul shrugged. "I thought it all was."

"Oh okay. I like being kissed, anyway, especially if I'm going to do the rest."

"Exactly! It shouldn't be all one way. You should demand what you want too, sweetheart. It's supposed to be about us all being satisfied, and that includes you."

I giggled. "Hmm. Okay, I'll like it if there's lots of kissing before the BJ."

# Paul

It was a hot afternoon and everyone went swimming in the new pond. My leg had healed enough to do the walk. Justine mostly sat under a tree reading a book for the third time. The guys left her alone there. Thomas returned to the cabin early to prepare the evening meal.

Jasper came from the pond and sat beside Justine. He didn't say anything. She continued reading. After a few minutes, he turned his head to watch her. She glanced a few times.

"What?" she asked finally.

He cupped her cheek and bent to her lips, kissing her softly. She leaned back on her hands, her book falling aside. Jasper deepened the kiss, probing a little at first then entering her mouth with his tongue.

Justine relaxed into his embrace. He continued mashing firmly and exploring her mouth. "Hey man," he said, peering back at me standing there watching.

"Hey," I replied, meeting Justine's eyes.

Jasper pressed to her lips again and re-inserted his tongue. He laid Justine down on her back and moved over her, pressing his bare chest to hers. She had on her big singlet with no panties. He felt down over her belly and cupped her crotch. Justine moaned as he forced his tongue in deep and gripped her pussy through the singlet. He rubbed her and clutched her inner thigh. She pressed her legs together but he got his hand between them and felt her pussy bare.

"Um Jasper!" she uttered in protest. "What are you doing?"

"You're so fucking hot," he said, and he kissed her again. "She's so fucking sexy, man," he said to me.

Justine gave in and relaxed her legs and let him feel into her pussy. He smeared her wetness and inserted his middle finger.

"I couldn't help overhearing you guys talking earlier – about kissing and letting us finger you," Jasper said to her. "Ooh that's tight. She's fucking tight, man." He grinned back at me.

Justine gripped the towel beneath her and lifted her hips to meet the insertions of Jasper's fingers. He was using two and sliding them in and out slowly. He continued searching her mouth with his tongue. She opened for him. He smoothed hair from her forehead and held the top of her head. He teased her mouth open wider and pressed his over it, his saliva dribbling in and making her swallow, and he delved deep into her mouth with his tongue again.

"Is this what you wanted, baby? You like being kissed, eh?"

"Uh huh, I like it."

"Don't know what's hotter, man, her mouth or her pussy."

"I think that's enough now," I said.

145

Justine grabbed hold of Jasper's arm and held it, grinding herself on his hand as her orgasm exploded through her. She clung to him. He held firmly up her. "Uhh..hhh now it's enough," she panted, rolling her eyes and biting her lip.

"Sorry man, I saw her sitting here reading and looking all sexy." Jasper rested on his side. He still had fingers in Justine's pussy. He spread them, opening her lips, then felt back up inside her.

I knelt, tilting my head to see. Justine waited while we both examined her. She had her legs bent up and partially open. Jasper extracted his fingers and spread her pussy lips again. "Love how wet they get after they cum, eh?"

"Yeah true," I said, shifting closer. I inserted two fingers. Justine watched my face. I met her gaze. She knew what I was thinking but I didn't know how she felt about it. I pulled down my boxers – it was all I was wearing. Justine parted her legs further and accepted me between them. I levered my cock down and pressed into her.

Jasper stood and watched me fuck my wife. It was quick. She seemed like she was on the verge of another orgasm but didn't quite get there before I thrust one last time and ejaculated.

Jasper was feeling his cock through his shorts. He dropped to his knees beside Justine's head. I got up off her, and she sat up a bit and took Jasper's cock into her mouth. He held her head and rolled his hips. She stroked him and sucked the swollen head. I watched in a daze as my wife's pretty mouth was being fucked, and she held my gaze while accepting the other man's load. She seemed to let it flood into her throat then she swallowed very deliberately, still holding my eyes.

She lifted from Jasper's cock and swallowed again. Then she squeezed until another drop of semen oozed from the tip, and she collected it with her tongue then sucked the tip again, probing the open eyelet and sucking out a little bit more cum. She held his dick up and kissed her way down the shaft to his balls. She cupped them with her other hand and moaned softly as she kissed each one.

Jasper held her head, softly caressing her. "Yeah take care of them, baby. That's right."

"Uh huh," Justine moaned as she sucked one of his balls half into her mouth and massaged with her tongue. She left off with a kiss and peered up. "Do you need to cum again?"

Jasper chuckled. "I think you drained them."

She smiled. "Good. But just for now, I hope."

"Oh yeah. You can fill them up again in the morning if you like."

"I like!" Justine looked to me. "Yummy!"

"Is it?"

"Yep. Not in the sweet tasting way."

"In what way, then?" Jasper was grinning huge.

Justine blushed. "Because it was *your* cum. Again! Bad boy."

"Love how you went for every last drop."

Jasper's pants were still around his knees. Justine lifted his flaccid penis and kissed the head. She squeezed the shaft and sucked, probing the eyelet with the tip of her tongue. He groaned and rolled his hips, his cock flexing and firming a little. Justine shut her eyes tight and took it into her mouth. She sucked the whole thing in. He was on the smaller side of average, out of proportion with the size of his testicles. She pulled back and lifted his dick to tend to them some more. "These are so amazing. I just love them."

I lifted her to her knees and mounted her. She took Jasper's cock back into her mouth, and I kept her body rocking so that it naturally surged in and out. Justine moaned through another orgasm just as I drove into her and held firm.

Jasper held the back of her head and fucked her mouth some more. Fully erect, he must have been a bit too long, so she closed her hand around his shaft, preventing him from entering too deeply. "Aw, fuck yeah!" he cried out and rammed his cock in as far as he could and held firm. "Yeah that's it, baby, drink it all down."

"Uh huh," Justine moaned, looking sideways at me as she again swallowed the other man's cum. She sucked off the end of his cock and kissed the tip. "Hmm was that nice, Jasper? Do you like me drinking your cum?" He pulled back down and thrust into her. Justine closed her eyes and sucked it. He pulled it out and rubbed her open mouth, teasing her with the swollen head. He lifted his shaft out of the way, and she kissed and softly sucked on his ball sac. "See, I knew they weren't quite empty before." She smiled across at me. "Now they are. And I hope yours are too!"

"Oh yeah. Mine are definitely empty."

"Mine have been sucked dry. I'm going for another swim," Jasper said and left.

Justine met my smile. "That was interesting."

"It was. It was frigging hot, sweetheart. You looked amazing doing that. I couldn't leave you alone."

"Did you like watching me?"

"It was incredible. Seeing his dick in your mouth like that – watching you take his load – that was frigging intense!"

Justine wrung her hands in front. "I loved you watching. It made me crazy."

"I wouldn't mind if he fucked you, sweetheart. I was thinking it and I would have liked it."

The idea pounded in my chest. I looked back over my shoulder at Jasper walking into the water. I hated the thought of it but knew it was only natural, with us all there stranded on an island together.

Justine nodded. "I know. I thought he was going to. I don't think there's any doubt Jasper is going to end up having me sooner or later. Mmm, he produces so much cum, and it tastes really strong. Imagine him servicing me with it properly..! Ooh, I love the thought of that. I'd love for you to watch him take me."

*Fuck yes, this had to happen!*

"Alright. I'll do it," I told my wife. "I'll watch him fuck you. But what about the others?"

"Uh huh, and them. It will be fun with Steven, and Thomas can have me tonight. I don't think either of them would like an audience, though. That would have to be in private, but Jasper's the main one, isn't he? He's the one you really want to see having actual intercourse with me?"

"Yeah, I guess. Like I said before, he's the one I see as competition for you. So, watching you pleasure him was intense, and I can only imagine how it will feel to see him doing you."

I imagined the guy nailing my wife. Imagined his arse pumping between her spread legs – him taking her from me – having to watch him own her, make her squeal.

Justine peered up through her blush. "And what about you-know-what? Us leaving it to nature this past few months has been exciting, but what about with these other men and no birth control? Have you thought about that, Paul?"

My face heated. I knew we had no condoms or anything of course. The idea of Justine taking creampies from these other men intrigued me.

"It crossed my mind," I said.

"And?"

"And, what do YOU think, baby? Would you be okay with the risk?"

Jeez I hoped she would be. I wanted the others to all spunk her. I definitely wanted that now we were thinking about going that far.

"I don't know. I wouldn't mind if we just didn't worry about it. I won't mind if I end up pregnant to one of them."

"Oh yeah?" I asked, my voice drying up, my chest tight. "You won't mind if you end up pregnant to one of them instead of me?"

My wife grimaced, blushing deeply now. "Maybe the most dominant man will actually get me. I wonder if it works like that if there's different men's sperm in me at that time. It would be just more of nature taking its course with all of us here together."

"Yeah – perfectly natural," I agreed quickly. "I think that's how I feel about it too." I smoothed Justine's hair from her face and kissed her softly. "I suppose there's every chance you will get pregnant if they all start fucking you."

"Uh huh," Justine moaned into my mouth. "I don't think anyone at home will be surprised, with one girl being stuck on an island with four men." She giggled. "I say from now on, all semen should be deposited in me. I'd love to take care of them all that way – to take everything they've got either between my legs or in my mouth." She moved close to whisper. "Or even from behind sometimes."

"Really? You said you didn't like it that time."

"I'm a girl. I'm allowed to change my mind."

***

# Part 3: We get her Pregnant

# Paul

Justine and I walked back to the cabin together, leaving Steven and Jasper swimming. I built a fire to heat the water so Justine could have her shower. She wore her short blue singlet and panties to dinner.

I had been to the toilet and stopped at the bottom of the steps, remaining in shadow. It was after dark. I could see by the moonlight that Justine was being held closely by Jasper. They were on the veranda. Thomas and Steven were inside doing the dishes. Jasper bent my wife back and kissed her. She moaned softly into his mouth. The kiss went on and on.

"But not every five minutes," Justine whispered.

"Yeah, but often, right? More than the others?"

"Yes. I'm going to be more strict with Thomas and Steven. You and Paul, of course, can have me whenever you want, within reason. Especially if you're talking about kissing."

"Yeah? And what about this?"

155

"Mmm yes, that too. You can play with them as much as you want but gently with my nipples. Not hard, okay?"

"Okay. Like that?"

"Uh huh. That's nice." Justine accepted another long, searching kiss. "And Paul and I were talking about something else too. We're going to tell everyone tonight, but it's more about you, anyway. We've decided that, um... Well, if you other men want, you can have me fully... Like, to take me to bed and be with me that way."

Jasper kissed her again. "And fuck you?"

"Uh huh if you want to."

He took her parted lips again, making her moan and begin to pant raggedly.

"But I still want to suck you sometimes. You have to let me."

Jasper chuckled. I deliberately coughed and made my presence known as I mounted the steps. Jasper turned and my wife stepped from behind him. She was straightening her hair. Her singlet was bunched up, her tits exposed beneath it.

"Justine was just saying you guys have decided to go all the way sharing, Paul. That's great. I was hoping you might."

"Yeah, after what happened at the pond this afternoon, we figured there wasn't much left to decide. I guess it makes us all equal here."

"True. It does. And I think it can work well – one woman satisfying four men. I mean, we might all be over-enthusiastic for the first couple of days, but over time we'll obviously be less demanding."

"I'll be fine," Justine said quickly. "I like being the only girl here. I'll try to keep all four of you satisfied. One way or another!" she added with a giggle.

"Do what *one way or another*?" Thomas asked, backing through the door with a tray of coffee cups.

Steven reached through and pushed the door open wider. Everyone set up around the veranda, sitting on chairs or on the steps.

"We were talking about having sex," Justine announced, belatedly answering Thomas's question. "Proper sex."

"Oh! This sounds good," Thomas ventured. "You mean..?"

"Yes. We don't see why not. It's already turned into a big sexy native holiday. Paul and I don't see why we should limit things in that way."

"Do you mean full sex?" Steven asked.

"Yes Steven, but only if you want to, of course. You don't have to do anything you don't want to do."

"I want to!"

Everyone laughed.

"You bet I want to!" the young guy added emphatically.

"And would you, Thomas?" Justine asked softly. "I wouldn't mind. I think I'd like it."

"I want to, love. I was hoping things might lead there. I agree this adventure is exhilaratingly natural. You complete that beautifully."

"Here, here!" Jasper toasted. "Absolutely beautifully." He chuckled. "Only next time I think we should do this in a little more style. A few conveniences would be nice."

"Next time, huh? Don't get too carried away," I challenged playfully, and everyone joined in another laugh.

"What if I shouted?" Jasper tossed back. "Nicer food and umbrella drinks!"

"And shampoo and conditioner!" Justine added. "And more underwear!"

"Aw, you being near naked is more than half the fun, though."

"Yeah, maybe for you guys."

"What about more women then?" Thomas asked.

Justine shook her head. "No, I'm the only woman allowed. I like being the only female with all you men."

"Ooh yeah!" Jasper cheered. "Now that we get to start fucking you."

"Uh huh exactly. You just have to share me, but I'm sure I can make it so you don't miss other women in that way."

"What about protection, love… the risk of pregnancy?" Thomas asked evenly.

"Um. Yes, there would be the risk of that," Justine uttered. "We've been unprotected for a few months now, and it hasn't happened yet."

"So, you've been trying to have a baby?"

"Not exactly. Just letting it happen if it did."

Jasper grinned. "I'd be happy to help."

Justine bit her lip. "Okay." She peered around at everyone. "I won't mind if it's one of you other men who gets me pregnant. You can all cum inside me. You won't need to pull out or anything."

"Fuck yeah," Jasper groaned.

Justine's blush intensified. "I can't wait actually. You men have been so strong for me here and make me feel so safe. It feels right that I should accept your sperm inside me." She blushed even more deeply as she peered around at us all. "I think you're all entitled to enjoy me and for me to worry about the semen all four of you need to produce each day. You can all just have sex with me and cum inside me... get me pregnant if that's what happens."

"I wanna cum inside you, Justine," Steven announced.

"Okay Steven, of course you can. I want you to," Justine offered sweetly. "I know you'll be able to nice and deep."

"He and I both," Thomas said, kneading Justine's shoulders.

"Uh huh, that's going to be interesting. I've never been done by anyone really huge before. You'll have to let me get used to it at first."

"I will love, don't worry. I'll do you nice and slow." He massaged down her front and felt her tits.

Everyone watched. I sat quietly while the older man met my wife's lips. He was feeling her firmly and tweaking her nipples. She was opening her mouth, and he was sticking his tongue in deep. He chuckled softly. "If only your father could see me now."

"Uh huh," Justine moaned into another kiss. "I wish he could too. I won't mind if he finds out. I hope everyone finds out you were all having me. I feel proud, not ashamed. It's perfectly reasonable with you men taking care of me here that you get to have turns servicing me sexually as well."

"That's right. It's perfectly natural," Jasper agreed. "Take care of the female – protect her – and she will be available to meet your needs."

I cleared my throat. Everyone looked to me. "That's how I'm looking at this. We're all taking care of each other, so you guys are all looking after Justine. I think it's only fair that you get to share her. And I guess there's every chance she'll end up pregnant from it, so when we get back home there'll probably be a story to tell. I don't think we need to be telling the newspapers that you were all servicing her that way, but if it comes up privately with friends and family, I don't mind us all talking about it."

"I don't care if my parents find out. I'm proud too," Steven declared, making Justine smile. "I'll be proud if it's me who gets you."

"Uh huh," Justine uttered through her blush, peering around. "I don't know when I'll actually be ovulating but you can all start trying to get me if you want."

"Okay then, are you ready, love?" Thomas asked her. He took her hand and led toward the cabin door.

"You guys have to stay out here," Justine said, smiling back.

I watched the door close. I sat quietly on the step while Jasper and Steven chatted. Minutes passed. I was mentally picturing what was happening inside – Justine actually being fucked by one of the other men for the first time.

I was feeling kind of spaced out and out of touch with reality right now. There was obviously every chance Justine would end up pregnant from this, and only a fraction of a chance the child would be mine. I didn't want to stop it though. I wanted her to keep sucking their cocks and swallowing their cum. I wanted them getting off in her mouth and up her cunt as well.

I wanted my wife with a constant creampie from these three other guys emptying their balls in her every day. I crushed my cock in my pants while thinking about that and listening through the door of the cabin.

After a good 20 minutes, all had remained silent inside.

## Justine

I held the older man's head, closing my thighs and flinching as his tongue swirled over my clit. It was too sensitive after my orgasm. He had two long bony fingers up me, pressed back against my G-spot. He extracted them and kissed his way up my belly to my breasts and to meet my lips. He was positioning himself as he kissed me. I guided his erect penis. I was slick and open. He penetrated me.

"Uhh..hh, that's deep."

"It's okay, love. Just relax. I'll be gentle."

I could handle his girth easily enough, but he was incredibly long. He started fucking me slowly, withdrawing a long way then inserting until the head of his cock was nudging my cervix. He held firm and pressed a little. I could feel the pressure, but he relented before it hurt too much.

"Is that okay, love?"

"Uh huh. A little bit like that's nice."

"Alright, I'll save it for when I'm ready to cum."

He held my head to his neck, his lower body settling into a faster rhythm but the penetration not so deep. I clung to him, his skin sort of soft and loose, his muscles tense. I cuddled to his body and went back into orgasm. He fucked me through it and into another before forcing his cock in deep again and holding firm.

My father's friend let out a throaty groan of pleasure. He was pressed hard against my opening, his dick all the way inside me, throbbing and gushing semen against my cervix. He quickly softened and the pressure released. He remained in me and kissed my lips. "It feels good to be all the way in like that when I cum, love. I hope it didn't hurt."

"No, it was fine. It felt nice."

Thomas lifted his upper-body to look at me in the moonlight. I kept my legs open for him as he continued slowly screwing me. He gradually firmed again. "I need to get another load off, love."

"Okay," I uttered.

He lay down on me and resumed humping more forcefully. I clung to him and waited. Finally he surged deep and held firm again, his old body taut and his penis throbbing, more of his cum spurting against my cervix.

"Ooh that's good, love. I really needed that after so long."

"Hmm, I suppose you're all going to be a bit horny," I said, giggling softly. "But I don't mind. You can keep having me as much as you need to for a while."

Thomas got up off me and stepped into his trousers. "Thanks love. So, tomorrow after dinner again?"

"Yes definitely." I pulled up my panties.

I was led back outside to the cheers of the other men. Paul met my smile. I sat with him and cuddled up, feeling quite strange with my pussy full of another man's cum. We were soon left alone outside.

Paul stroked my hair. "Are you okay?"

"I'm fine. I've really been unfaithful now, though," I said softly. "I've had full, unprotected sexual intercourse with another man, and he came inside me twice."

"Twice huh?"

"Uh huh – and deep – really deep!"

"Yeah, I kind of figured by his package," Paul said. "He's that big, is he?"

"Yes. Not that it means anything, but he's much longer than anyone who has had me before. I couldn't take him comfortably, only when he was ready to cum. Then he forced it all the way in." I whispered teasingly, "He was inside me a lot deeper than you've ever been, Paul."

Paul met my lips. "Yeah? And twice, huh?"

"Uh huh. Both times he forced it in so hard it felt like the head of his dick was poking into my belly. But I'm not dripping at all, which is good." I whispered close to my husband's ear. "His sperm is in my womb, Paul. I've been serviced with another man's baby making goo."

My husband groaned anxiously. I loved him having to deal with this and accept it. "Oh god I can still feel him on top of me and so deep inside," I whispered, teasing some more. "I feel so alive as a woman right now, Paul... I can't wait to be a woman for Jasper and let him fuck me and cum inside me... I can't wait to be a girlfriend for Steven and let him spear me with that huge long pole he's got..!"

## Paul

I went to the toilet before going inside, the idea of Justine's womb being alive with old Thomas's sperm making my face hot. When I entered the cabin, I disturbed Jasper kissing Justine. The guy lifted from her. She sat up on the couch, wiping her mouth on the back of her hand. She had a book. Jasper left her and sat at the table where a new hand of cards had been dealt.

I joined in the game, and after a while Justine went to her bed. "Goodnight, everyone."

Everyone said goodnight and watched her. She didn't close her curtain. She lifted her top off and lay down on her back in the moonlight, pulling her sheet to her waist.

"That's nice, eh?" Jasper said.

"Beautiful," Thomas agreed.

"Except it's still too hot," Justine complained. "Could you get me a drink please, Steven?"

Steven took her a glass of water. She sat up and drank some. He stood looking down at her. Jasper and Thomas were still playing the hand of cards. I watched young Steven sit on the edge of the bed. He leaned in and kissed Justine's lips. "Oh," she uttered in surprise, and she rested back on her hands as he bent to her again.

The other two men turned to watch as well. Steven kissed Justine passionately and felt her tits. She lay back and he lay beside her, still kissing and feeling her. He reached down over her belly and beneath the sheet. "Uhh..hhh," Justine panted. "Not too rough, okay?"

"Okay," Steven said, and he looked back at what he was doing, his arm lifting then moving forward.

"Uhh…hhh," Justine moaned softly.

"Should I go in and out?" Steven asked her.

"Yes, slowly. You can use two fingers if you want… Uhh..hhh yes, like that."

"Can I suck your tits too?"

"Okay." Justine lifted her chest as he bent to her. I noticed her legs were open. The sheet gradually slipped and revealed Steven's arm just moving slightly back and forth, his fingers squelching wetly inside her as he sucked on one nipple then the other. She soon gripped his arm and writhed onto her side, panting and moaning.

"Are you okay?" Steven asked.

Justine giggled. "Yes. You just made me orgasm."

"Oh. You're really slippery now."

"I know. It's normal."

"It means she's ready to take your dick inside," Jasper explained. "It's her body lubricating her vagina for sex."

Steven nodded, taking that in. He turned to Justine. "But has it been too much already today for you? Do you wanna go to sleep?"

"I'm fine, Steven. You can have sex with me if you want."

Steven grinned.

Justine looked to me, biting a lip. "Can you close the partition for us, please?"

I slid the curtain across and watched from the edge of it until Steven had pulled down his pants and gotten into bed with Justine. I caught a quick flash of the young guy's dick, which was incredibly long.

Jasper and Thomas went back outside. I sat on the couch and listened to my wife being fucked. The cot was squeaking, and she had to tell the guy to be careful not to hurt her a few times. It sounded like he was losing it, so I went back to the edge of the curtain and watched.

"Uhh..hh," Justine cried softly as Steven thrust hard between her legs and held firm, his bottom clenched and his toes hooked around the base of the cot. "Oh that's so deep, Steven."

"Aw yeah, you're so hot inside," he groaned, and he squirmed against her, thrusting around. "Thanks for letting me fuck you, Justine. It's so great."

"Thank YOU, Steven. You gave me another orgasm, you know?" She kissed him softly. "You have such a nice cock. I love how deep inside me you came just then."

"You're even more slippery now. It feels nice sliding in and out like this."

"Uh huh, I like it too. Keep kissing me while you do it."

He kissed her and kept thrusting. "But I'm gonna cum again if I keep going."

"That's okay, just let it go inside me."

I sat back on the couch and just listened to the cot squeaking – listen to my wife with her legs spread and her cunt being reamed by my young cousin. It was quite a while before Steven cried out and was obviously blowing his second load in her. Pumping it directly into her womb, I imagined. After that all was quiet, and I checked to find them both asleep, my wife cuddled in the young guy's arms.

I went to bed. The other men came in later, and the cabin was in silence. I saw Steven climbing up to the loft in the early hours of the morning. When I woke after sunrise, I heard Justine's cot squeaking and peeped around the edge of the curtain to meet her eyes. Jasper was thrusting toward his climax. He held firm and groaned his release. Justine held his head close and had her other hand on his hip as she accepted his deposit of semen into her pussy.

Jasper followed Justine's gaze to smile up at me. "Just getting a shot off, man. Figured I'd better get onto her early if I wanted to go first today."

I swallowed. "Yeah, fair enough."

Justine's blush intensified but Jasper kissed her and resumed humping slowly. He looked back at me but included Justine as he spoke, "It's good we don't have to worry about pulling out or anything. All good with us getting her pregnant then, eh?"

My face heated as I exchanged a look with my wife. "Yeah, I guess there's every chance," I admitted.

Justine took a breath and looked to Jasper. "I want to have a baby anyway." She blushed a bit. "I mean we were planning to, so…"

Jasper stopped thrusting and rested there smiling. "Yeah?"

I swallowed hard again and nodded. "If it's one of you guys who actually get her, we'll just have to accept that and live with it is all."

Jasper's smile broadened. "Fuck yeah! Fucking definitely. I'd love to knock you up, baby."

"Okay. And I'd really love it to be you," Justine gushed.

I huffed, expelling a nervous breath. "But it will still be an island baby – just sort of natural that there'll be more of a chance that one of you guys will be the father."

"Yeah I get that, man," Jasper agreed, lifting to look down at where he was still inside Justine. "Makes perfect sense to me."

# Justine

I poured my tea and approached the breakfast table where all four men were seated. I bit down on my grin. "Well, it didn't take long for you all to have me."

"Regrets, love?" Thomas asked.

"No, none. It's nice. I feel so close to each of you now. So intimate."

Thomas pulled me close as I leaned against him sitting. He stroked up my outer-thigh to my hip. I edged onto his lap in my short singlet and panties.

"You're not too sore this morning, love?"

"No, I'm fine. I know you men had been waiting."

I was so pleased to have had them all inside me. To have given them all the pleasure of taking me fully.

"Well, we're all drained now," Jasper said and chuckled. "We all are, aren't we, men?"

"I am," Steven said.

"Me too," Thomas agreed, grinning.

Paul put up a hand. "Same."

I smiled through my blush. "Well, it sounds like I'm doing my new job then, doesn't it?"

Jasper claimed my foot as I pressed it against his knee. He held it and massaged my calf. "Filling all of our balls and emptying them for us sounds like a fair enough job to me. What do you think, Paul, that's what you call sharing, eh buddy?"

"Yeah it is," Paul replied evenly. "As long as it doesn't get to be too much. It's up to Justine if she can't take one of you at any time."

"Of course!" Thomas declared. The other two agreed.

"It won't get to be too much, though," I said. "Now that you're all actually fucking me, I don't mind how often, or even if you wanted to go one after the other or watch each other." I bit down on my grin again. "I'm sure I can take it as much as the four of you can do me."

"Fuck yeah," Jasper groaned.

"Does it matter how much semen you have inside?" Steven asked curiously. "Can there be too much?"

"Physically there's no limit, Steven," Thomas answered. "There's no reason a woman can't accept multiple ejaculations from a group of men. There's nothing unhealthy about that. It's just sperm and seminal fluid, isn't it love?"

"Uh huh. The worst of it will be that I drip a bit sometimes, if there's too much. But that's nothing for you men to worry about. It's just a part of my new job, to accept any deposit of cum any of you want to make in me. Anytime any of you need to get off, you can do it in my belly or in my mouth." I peered around at the three other men and my husband. "Just pretend I'm your girl and you can have me whenever you want."

"Hello there!" suddenly boomed a voice from outside. "Anyone home?"

"What the fuck?" Jasper cried, jumping to the open door.

There was an islander man, smiling. "Well I'll be damned," he said, looking in the door. "You're the plane crash people?"

"We are," Thomas replied. "We've been here a month. You know about us?"

"We heard about a search a long way south. I knew they should have tried up here," he said. "They called it off a few weeks ago, but they never came this far north."

I was hiding behind the men – behind Steven and Jasper. Steven touched my side, keeping me from view of the islander man while they spoke. It seemed he was responsible for running supplies to the cabin for the company of meteorologists who camped here every year for a few months. He occasionally checked on the place through the summer and autumn because of the storms, to make sure the cabin was not damaged and his supplies ruined.

I snuck back to my room and put on my sundress. I went back out and made my way forward to meet the man who had rescued us. He was from an island about three hours away. He had his boat with plenty of room for everyone. We would be safely back in civilisation by lunchtime, he had explained cheerily. He was a jolly character, not at all worried about us having ravaged his supplies.

Thomas made coffee, and the man, Loco, got some sweet biscuits from his boat for everyone. It was a simple thing but quite the luxury after a month on rations. After a while chatting and laughing, the men all got to work bringing up the supplies Loco had and filling the diesel tank with the fuel he'd brought. They started the generator and got the fridge and freezer working. He needed to give them a run every few months.

"I'm kind of sad that we're leaving," I confessed to Jasper when we were alone in the cabin.

"I know, it's been good here," he agreed. "It's been something unexpected that I think I really needed. I'm certainly going to appreciate all the little things we take for granted from now on."

"Me too," I said. "It's been nice just feeling nature and not having to deal with everything. I almost wish this man hadn't come for another month."

"I'm glad he didn't come yesterday!" Jasper said and grinned.

I blushed. I couldn't help it. "I know! But I was going to be the girl for you men. Now I'm just going to be one of the many girls that all men have to think about and want. It's hard not to feel disappointed actually."

178

Jasper nodded. "So, it will be good to get back though, right? Good to get back to friends and family?"

"I suppose. It will be good to call my parents and tell them I'm alive. They must be so worried."

"Good to get back to work too?" Jasper teased.

"Um no, not really." I giggled. "I haven't missed work at all."

Jasper laughed too. "Yeah, your dad would have everything under control. He would have had to take on some of the work at first but he would have brought in some temporary help. I'm sure it's all cruising along by now."

Paul came in and sat down with me at the table, squeezing my hand. Jasper stepped behind me and massaged my shoulders. "We were just saying how it's a shame to be rescued in a way, man. Things were just getting fun, eh?"

Paul nodded. "True." He met my eyes. "I kind of wish we could have done this for a while now that we've started."

I blushed again. "You mean sharing me?"

179

"Yeah I guess. It was kind of crazy but interesting."

Jasper grinned. "What if we just pretend this guy didn't find us yet? What if we all go with him today and call home then pick up some nicer food and drink and come back? How would that be?"

"What! Really?" I cried. "Are you serious?"

"Yeah. Well, we've been stuck here on rations so far. Why not finish off with a more fun couple of weeks before we leave? We've got power now. We can have fresh fruit and umbrella drinks!"

"Umbrella drinks?" I giggled. Jasper was still massaging my bare shoulders and making me tingle all over.

"You could still be the girl," he breathed into my hair. "We could get Thomas and Steven to come back too, and you could be the girl for all of us for a few weeks or so... We could go shopping at this guy's village. He said there's a big mall and that. We could take my credit card for a spin and get whatever you want – except clothes – you have to still let us look," he teased.

I held my husband's gaze as Jasper reached down the front of my dress and felt my breast. He tilted my head back and kissed me, searching my mouth with his tongue while tweaking my nipple.

"I'll leave you guys to talk," he said, breaking off the kiss, and he removed his hand from down my dress and went outside to the other men.

*

"It's an interesting idea," Paul said. "I don't suppose there's any reason we need to hurry home. We could have been stranded here for months anyway."

I squeezed my husband's hands across the table. "I wonder if Steven and Thomas will want to stay. It would be great if we all did, don't you think?"

"I'd be surprised if they didn't want to, sweetheart. Considering what would be on offer, that is."

I blushed some more. "You mean..!"

"Yeah, I mean my sexy wife being on offer. As if they're going to knock back a chance to fuck you again. They know there's no chance of this happening back home."

"I know. It can only happen here," I agreed. "It sounds like Jasper really wants to do it. He gets so passionate when he's kissing me, have you noticed?"

"Yeah, I noticed. It would be a shame to stop now that everything's just become so open. I mean, I've just started getting used to him getting with you like that. I think I'd like it to go on for a while – to let him fuck you regularly for a few weeks."

"Uh huh," I uttered. "I'd like that too, and with Thomas and Steven. It's so amazing how deep they both penetrate me. I'd love to experience that again. Or over and over again!" I added, biting my lip. "Especially now that I'll be able to shop for some things. I'll be able to make myself more attractive for them – to feel and smell pretty and wash my hair properly."

"To make yourself all beautiful for them, huh?"

"Uh huh. That way Jasper might want me even more," I said teasingly. "He could even sleep with me some nights if you want. Mmm, cuddling me fully naked and screwing me with you just the other side of the curtain." I reached under the table and pressed my husband's package with my toes. He was fully erect. "Mmm let's stay, okay? I'll be the plaything for all of them but especially for Jasper."

"Yeah, but why do I like the idea? That's the only problem I have. I don't get why I want them to keep fucking you, baby. I definitely do! I hope Jasper can work it out with this islander guy so we can stay for a while longer. I think another few weeks or a month would be good."

I smiled. "Mmm, I like the sound of that. Another month would be perfect." I held my husband's gaze. "I think it's just because we've all been getting around half naked – the reason we want to be sexy. It feels so natural being the only female with four men. I know I feel completely wanton like this. Maybe you're picking up on that and you feel excited to see me this way. I was thinking about it last night, and I can imagine how it would be for you guys as well – the female ready to be taken by each of you. It must be nearly as exciting to watch as it is to actually be the one having me. I know I love the idea of you watching each other."

I so wanted them to watch each other taking me. I wanted to be a complete slut and for them all to see me that way. I would even let the islander man fuck me if they wanted him to – maybe if it would help do a deal with him. He could have sex with me as payment for taking us to his island and back.

Paul was nodding to what I'd said about them watching each other with me. "Yeah, that's all true, baby. It's exactly like that."

I just blushed again. "And I really don't mind if everyone back home finds out, you know Paul? I kind of hope the others brag about it. I won't be embarrassed... Well, I might, but in an exciting way."

"Well, even if we leave today they all got onto you. They've got plenty to brag about already."

"Will you tell them again they're allowed to? They might if you say it's okay."

There were footsteps on the veranda. Thomas came in and went to the kitchen. "This is exciting, isn't it? Rescued!"

"It's good to know we're not going to be stuck here and run out of supplies at least," Paul agreed.

Thomas finished his glass of water and approached. "That generator sounds good, doesn't it? Lights – refrigeration!"

I smiled back up at him as he claimed my shoulders.

He looked from me to Paul. "Jasper was saying you were thinking about staying a while longer."

"Yeah, though it would depend on whether we were allowed to."

"Yes, that's what Jasper's about to ask the guy, Loco. I think he might be okay with it, as long as we pay for everything to be restocked and make it worth his while to taxi us to do our shopping."

Paul nodded. "We were thinking about three or four more weeks – for fun now, though."

Thomas massaged my shoulders. "And with our new arrangement continuing?" he asked.

"Yes. With that," Paul answered evenly. "Are you interested in staying on too, Thomas?"

"Yes, of course!" He was grinning down at me. I blushed some more. He bent to me, and I met his lips. He inserted his tongue and slipped a hand down my dress to feel a breast. He broke off the kiss. "We'll need to call home and let the authorities know so they can recover bodies and investigate the plane crash."

I cuddled his arm, keeping it in place as he played with my nipple. My dress hung from my shoulder. I got up and slipped onto Thomas's lap as he sat down. His arm was around my waist, and he continued casually fondling my nipple while we chatted about what we would need to buy.

## Jasper

Justine came out onto the veranda of the cabin with her dress off one shoulder and hanging down that arm. She lifted her arms to rake at her hair but that didn't fix it. The islander guy who had found us had already seen her and his eyes had lit up, I noticed. I figured our one female plane-wreck survivor was a trump card to be played if this guy didn't want to let us stay on here in the cabin. Since all four of us men were fucking Justine now, I figured we could offer her to him as well if needed, but let's see if I could talk him around first with the offer of cash instead.

Young Steven and I were helping him unload his boat onto the jetty. There were quite a lot of supplies to stock the cabin. We all sat to rest and I tried asking straight up. "So Loco, how would it be if we actually didn't want to leave right away? I mean, if we wanted to stay on for another few weeks or a month or so – could that be arranged?"

The guy grinned. "Cost you, man. It's my camp – you got money?"

"I've got money." I nodded. "Money's no worries at all."

He smiled bigger. "No one's here until June. I can do a run each week for a thousand plus the cost of the supplies."

"Yeah? And can you take us with you today and bring us back tonight or tomorrow?"

"Another two thousand," the guy calculated. "One thousand each trip. Here and back, here and back is two thousand. We come back tomorrow!"

"Tomorrow's good. Is there a hotel?"

Loco nodded. "Nice one! You got more money?" He grinned again.

"I've got more money." I chuckled. "What about a satellite phone, they work out here? Do you know where I can get one?"

"No problem, man. We get one today. More money!"

"Yeah, yeah, more money!" I laughed.

I went to find the others up in the cabin packing their few possessions.

"Okay we're good to stay on. Loco's going to take us to his island today and bring us back tomorrow. Apparently there's a nice hotel. Then he'll be doing supply runs for us each week for as long as we stay."

"Wonderful," Thomas said and went to the kitchen.

"That's good," Paul agreed.

I took hold of Justine from behind. She leaned back against me as I kissed her neck. "And you're still going to be our girl, are you? You're going to look after us all?"

"Uh huh," Justine uttered. "I'm going to be the girl for you all. You can make pretend-love to me as much as you want. I'll try not to say no too often."

"Damn, you were hot this morning, baby," I breathed into her ear, loud enough that her husband heard. I fucking loved the fact they were married and we were getting onto his wife in front of him. "She's a good fuck, man. Nice and tight, and she cums so easily," I said to him.

"True," he agreed, making Justine's blush fire up.

She reached back and held my neck while I felt her tits. I pinched her nipples through her dress, holding them and grinding against her bottom. She arched and wiggled back against my package. I hugged her and reached one hand down to cup her between the legs. I was under the skirt of her dress and feeling her through her panties. She bit her lip and held her husband's gaze as I slipped my hand down the front of them and opened her pussy. "Uh huh," she moaned softly as I inserted a finger.

"Yeah so fucking tight, man," I said to the guy. I guided his wife back onto my lap and felt up inside her. He was just standing there watching. Justine lifted the skirt of her dress so he could see. She gathered it and held it bunched against her belly while I fingered her.

Thomas approached and stood by the door, keeping watch for the islander man. He would glance outside then turn back to watch what I was doing. Justine met his eyes and blushed a bit deeper.

I lifted from nuzzling her neck to kiss her lips. She closed her eyes and opened for my tongue. I searched her mouth, my middle finger embedded in her and rubbing back against her G-spot.

As soon as I built up another load I'd be fucking the hot little slut again. Pounding her nice and hard and pumping more baby batter into her womb. I'd be the one knocking her up, nothing surer. I looked at her husband watching while that thought went through my mind and pulsed in my balls. It was as if he heard what I was thinking, the way his face flushed from pale to red.

"They're coming," Thomas said.

"Yeah, we'd better help lug some more of those supplies up here anyway," I replied.

I had left Justine's mouth wet. She wiped it on her wrist as she held her husband's eyes again. I was smoothing her panties back into place.

I sucked my finger. "Damn, that tastes more like me than you," I said with a chuckle, and I kissed Justine again. "Does that taste like cum?"

She shrugged. "I don't know, a little bit."

"You're not going to be getting any birth control when we're in town eh?" I looked from the girl to her husband, smirked. "Another four weeks… we're definitely going to have her fucked pregnant for you, buddy."

Paul gulped and glared back at me. He nodded stiffly. "Yeah I guess." He took a breath, nodded some more. "And probably every chance it will be you who gets her."

"Haha true that." I smoothed hair over his wife's ear. "I'll be pumping another load into her every chance I get. Make sure her womb's full of my sperm at all times, eh baby."

"Mmm it certainly feels like it is," she uttered into another kiss. "I hope it's him that gets me," she said to her husband and Thomas. "You can all cum inside me each day

191

but I'll be hoping it's Jasper that gets me pregnant... I'd love to have his baby," she directed squarely at her husband.

Old Thomas gripped the husband's shoulders. "Oh son," he consoled.

"No it's okay. I want it to happen too," he said and gulped hard again. "I want you all to keep fucking her and especially you, Jasper. Make sure she's full of your seed each night when she goes to bed, or even take her to bed sometimes and do her through the night... Try and get her pregnant, man. Try and get my wife pregnant!"

# Justine

An hour later, I was standing at the back of the small cabin cruiser. I had on my sundress and tennis shoes. I had to keep hold of the skirt of my dress to stop it from being lifted by the wind. I had noticed the islander man looking at me a few times – at my legs and down the front of my dress. My two older boyfriends had joined me at the back of the boat with the islander guy, Paul and Steven busy driving and talking.

I noticed Thomas and Jasper both watching my legs a bit so I released the skirt of my dress and let it flutter in the wind and sometimes lift up against my stomach. I was leaning back against a rail and didn't try to fix it as it folded up and stuck there for a while.

Thomas and Jasper were both staring at my panties. I was thinking about the fact my belly was all warm with their sperm. "I hope you men are still feeling satisfied now," I said to them. "I hope it's been a nice release for you both so far."

"It was a full release for me," Jasper replied. "I'm very satisfied."

I smiled through my blush, pleased to hear he'd called it a full release. It had certainly felt like it when he was cumming in me that last time.

"Me too love." Thomas moved beside me and put an arm around my shoulders. "You really drained my old balls," he said into my ear.

"Mmm that sounds nice. I hope I really did. I guess that's all you men need sometimes, isn't it? To have your girlfriend take care of that for you. Or your pretend girlfriend." I giggled. "I'm actually sorry I made you wait so long now," I went on softly with them both leaning close from either side. "I should have been taking better care of you weeks ago. Being the only girl, I should have been keeping your boys busy all the time – filling them and emptying them for you – making them feel nice and active."

"Yeah, filling them and emptying them is the way," Jasper said, smoothing my hair aside and kissing my lips softly. "The more full you can get them before blowing the better."

He kissed me softly a second time and I peered around shyly, making sure the two up the front weren't watching. I blushed at Thomas's grin then turned back to Jasper.

"So, did I get yours full enough that first time? It was a lot to swallow."

"You did, baby. You filled them real nice," Jasper said, grinning in reply.

"And waiting for it was fine too, love," Thomas said. "It made it pretty exciting."

I smiled. "So is waiting better or would you prefer to have me when you want?"

"Waiting was exciting," Jasper replied.

"Yeah for me too," Thomas agreed. "I like our sharing plan."

"Hmm well, I was thinking if I have a nice hotel room for tonight that it would be fun to have some special visits," I said to them. "Maybe after my bath, if I can have one. Maybe for an hour or so each, and you two could work out who's first and surprise me? It would be nice to be made love to just one time by you both in a real bed."

They both nodded and exchanged glances.

"But it will also be nice to actually sleep in a real bed, so you can only have an hour each, and then you have to go away and leave me alone!" I added defiantly. "And Steven doesn't need to know either. He wouldn't appreciate a soft bed anyway, so he can wait until we get back to the island for his next turn."

Jasper grinned. "Clean sheets – you completely naked – perfect!"

"Uh huh," I uttered. "With me naked and with you men actually on top of me! I really love the feel of a man on top of me. His strong, heavy body pressing me into the bed while he's doing me."

"Aw fuck," both men groaned.

*

The island Loco took us to was a modern tourist destination. There were resorts, beach-front hotels and the full shopping experience. It was also on-season being summer, so there wasn't a lot of available accommodation to pick from. There was one upper-level room at a five-star hotel on the beach that the men offered to me and Paul. The men left me there to freshen up and do some shopping while they went to find rooms for themselves and call their families and organize the supplies they would need. They wanted red meat and beer. I put in my order for lots of fresh fruit and vegetables, which I had been really missing. I also wanted umbrella drinks and left it up to Jasper to be barman when we got back to the island. He liked the idea and promised to surprise me with different cocktail drinks.

I called my mother and cried on the phone with her for ages before telling her not to worry and that I would be perfectly safe staying on my tropical island for a few more weeks. I also called a few close friends.

My room had a spa-bath that would wait a few hours until I had done my shopping. I had a nice long shower and wore my sundress and tennis shoes. Jasper had offered me money but I didn't need it. He was paying for everything else, and I only needed to buy a few things to wear and some basic toiletries – shampoo, conditioner, deodorant and perfume, a new brush and some hair clips and ties, some tampons and some skin creams and the like, and a bit of make-up. I bought some more underwear and a few skirts and tops, and some nighties. I found a few pairs of sandals and a couple of sunhats.

I got to thinking about the men I was staying on this desert island with as I relaxed in my room after shopping. I felt differently about each of them: Steven was younger, and it felt quite wrong to be with him, but wrong in an exciting way. Jasper was a confident and attractive man, and someone I now saw as directly in competition with my husband. He was very much *another man*. Thomas was a parental figure. I had known him as long as I could remember and had only recently agreed to stop calling him Mr Griffon. I felt truly loved and very much cared for by him. Pleasuring him with my mouth and hand earlier and then allowing him between my legs felt like giving in to something that he has been wishing for all along. I was so pleased that he was there when the plane crashed and stranded us. He made me feel safe and reassured. I was more than happy to let him have his wish and offer him the use of my vagina and mouth, or just to feel and look at my breasts whenever he felt like it.

# Paul

I left my wife to her thoughts and went down to the bar in the lobby of the hotel, where I found our alpha-male group leader sipping a cold beer. It felt a little different being here in civilisation, but we were still a long way from home and on a tiny remote island with no one we knew around. Our little plane-wreck survivor group was still intact and Jasper was definitely still in charge.

"How's our girl going, man, she get her shopping done?" he asked.

"Yeah she's all good. Got everything she needs."

I nodded, sipped the beer the barman had served me.

"We want to fuck her in her bed tonight, buddy. Did she say?"

I nodded again. "Yeah, she said."

"Haha good. It'll be nice fucking her on a proper mattress for a change. But you'd know that, eh man. Being married to her and all... I've often wondered just watching her around the office whether she'd be a good fuck. It's been interesting on the island like this but it's going to be more like reality taking your wife to an actual bed."

"Yeah I guess... She said she wants to have a bath and be all soft and smelling pretty for you."

"Oh yeah?" The guy smirked. "Bit like fucking your bride on her wedding night, eh!"

He held my gaze steadily. I felt my face flushing.

I swallowed hard. "Yeah it feels a bit like that," I admitted. "This hotel kind of reminds me, I suppose. Plus with the way she's talking about shaving her pussy for you, like she did for me that night."

"Ah good, shaving it bald yeah?"

I nodded and took a breath. "So we can all see it better and you guys can enjoy the feel of it."

"Fuck yeah, perfect! And how about this islander guy, Loco, are we going to let him have a fuck of Justine too, man?"

"Um…" I felt my face flush again.

"It might help grease the wheels. Get him running back and forth after us with any supplies."

"Yeah I suppose… Although I wouldn't want him getting her pregnant. I'd rather that was you or Thomas, or Steven."

"Yeah true. Wouldn't want the guy knocking our girl up," Jasper agreed, sipping his beer. "Maybe just get her to give him blowjobs."

I nodded and shut up and let Jasper talk. He went on about our supply situation, as we had spent the afternoon stocking up and getting things to the boat ready to head back to the island in the morning. I kept thinking about it and didn't mind the idea of getting Justine to give this islander guy blowjobs. I liked the fact she was going to be sucking off these other men as well as letting them fuck her. It was exciting to think of her with their cocks in her mouth and swallowing their cum. I imagined sometimes she would be just jerking us off and taking the load at the end. Just getting us close and letting us empty our balls in her mouth. The thought of her doing that for this islander guy was interesting too.

That night she came downstairs for dinner with her tits bare and available for viewing down her dress. She had on her little red dress she had picked out for the Christmas party. The guys were all over her and getting her to pose for pictures, now that Thomas had been able to charge his phone.

I sat there throughout dinner and afterwards letting them work my wife and get her ready for them to fuck again. You could see her cunt was wet the whole time through her little white panties, which her dress barely covered.

I was so into this now though. I wanted it to happen and was boned up in my pants under the table when Justine took Steven upstairs. He was going first, although just getting a blowjob, as Justine whispered to me.

An hour later Thomas went up for his turn and another hour after that, Jasper left me drinking and went up to the room to fuck my wife as well. He'd lost the call with Thomas and had to go seconds this time.

I hung around the bar chatting with some locals and ended up seriously drunk by the time I went upstairs in the early hours and crawled into bed with my wife.

She was sweaty and I could smell the other men on her. I was reeling inside, my heart thumping. I was drunk enough to do this and kissed my way down her bare belly. She was half asleep and moaned at me, clutching a fistful of my hair. "Mmm Paul..!"

"Uh baby you're so fucking sticky," I groaned and kissed her tacky mons and nuzzled for her clit.

The bed was soaked beneath her. I pried her thighs open and buried my head between them, licking into her and sucking on her folds. She twisted my hair but relaxed her legs open wider for me. I licked the taste of them from her skin then peeled her open, pausing to see inside her with the light from the ensuite.

"They came in you again?" I asked. "This is from them both?"

Justine swallowed. "Uh huh."

"Damn it baby, it's everywhere. You're so fucking creamy inside."

"Mmm they came really hard, but they needed it," my wife uttered, thrusting and grinding her cunt up at me. "Mmm lick it, Paul... I want you to."

"Aw fuck," I groaned and tentatively touched a glob of white goo with a pointed tongue. I peeled my wife open further and saw it was a trickle from a thick pool of the stuff. "Who was last baby, Thomas or Jasper?"

"Um Jasper. But he came more than once."

"Oh right." I gulped and took a breath. I must have been sobering up fast because my head had cleared enough to think about this. I was sort of glad it was from Jasper rather than the old guy somehow. That thought occurred to me as I licked at the pool of goo. It was really thick and jelly-like. I collected it with my tongue and softly sucked it into my mouth and swallowed it.

The strong salty taste filled my senses. My wife moaned and kept hold of my hair as she ground herself against my mouth. I closed my eyes and probed deep into her, searching out more of the taste of these other men and licking and sucking it out of her. I could smell her juices too but there was no mistaking the taste of semen.

"Mmm that's so sexy Paul."

I swallowed and took a breath. "Yeah I guess… There's so much of it," I said and gathered another thick glob oozing from in deep. I spread my wife's labia wide open and sucked on her reddened tunnel. I swallowed another big gooey wad of pussy juice and cum, wondering whether I was still eating Jasper's semen or was it Thomas's now. I didn't care anymore and just wanted to clean it all out of my wife."

"Mmm it's all over your mouth," she said and pulled me up from between her legs. She licked my face and kissed me. "Mmm you taste like them Paul, that's so sexy," she moaned and kissed me some more.

I kissed her back, ravaging her open mouth and sharing the taste of these other men's semen with her. We collapsed cuddled together and I went to sleep with the scent of it thick on my breath and the taste coating my teeth and lining my throat.

I woke a few hours later to my wife smiling down at me with a coffee in her hand. I immediately remembered what I'd done. She was obviously thinking about it too. I made a face at the horrible taste still in my mouth.

"Uh huh tell me about it!" she teased, not offering the coffee yet.

I swallowed hard, grimacing as I sat up.

"Mmm that was so strong in your mouth, Paul, can you still taste it?"

I gulped again. "Yeah."

My wife smiled more tease. "And do you want to wash it down or do you like it?"

I took the cup of coffee. Drew a breath. "It wasn't so bad... I could taste you too."

I sipped my coffee. Justine sat and sipped hers too.

"I won't mind if you want to do that again next time," she said sweetly. "Anytime while we're doing this..."

I took another breath and nodded. "Okay baby, I'll do it sometimes, but as long as they don't find out okay?"

# Justine

Throughout the morning and trip back to our island, I was kissed and felt up a few times by each of the men but not serviced at all. They were lugging all the supplies up from the boat to the cabin. I was alone in the cabin for a moment and saw Jasper approaching with the short islander man. They were carrying the box with my bathtub in it. The other men were headed back to the boat for more supplies.

My heart was pounding with excitement for what I had in mind. I checked again and waited until they were approaching the steps, then I went to the wash tub and pushed down my panties and lifted off my dress. The men were laughing together as they came through the open door. I had hold of a towel but just clutched it in my hand and remained facing them as they stopped laughing and looked at me.

"Fuck yeah that's better, baby," Jasper said.

I blushed fully as I watched the islander man's face. He looked from my pussy to my breasts then back down at my pussy. "Ooh that's nice... Tight, yeah?" he asked Jasper but quickly looked back down at my crotch.

"Ooh yeah, she's tight alright," Jasper told the man. "Don't cover up, baby. Let him have a look."

I took a breath, just biting on my lip as they put down the box and approached. Jasper moved around behind me, stroking down my arms and claiming my wrists. He held them behind my back while the islander man bent down a little to look more closely at my pussy. Jasper held my wrists in one of his hands and felt my breasts with the other, tweaking my nipples and making my pussy tingle.

The islander man looked up at what Jasper was doing then motioned outside. "You all..?" he asked.

"Yeah we're all doing her, man. She likes it, eh! She's easy – anyone who wants some. Anytime!"

"Ah!" the smaller man exclaimed, his eyes wide and his white teeth showing with a huge smile.

I whispered back to Jasper, "You can give me to him if you want – to help pay for the boat trips."

"Yeah? You'll let him have a fuck?" Jasper returned evenly and kissed me.

"Yes," I uttered into his mouth. "If it helps with the payment."

Jasper looked down at the guy. "What do you say, Loco – sound fair?"

"Yes – fair." Loco was nodding enthusiastically. "Half payment plus the girl, yes?"

Jasper looked over his shoulder and checked out the window. "Okay – fifteen minutes!" he said to the islander man. He then kissed my neck. "We'll just let him have a quick fuck. I'll wait outside the door, okay?"

"Uh huh," I uttered. My mind was numb, my legs rubbery and my entire body tingling hot like my face.

Jasper left me standing there and went to the door. He checked back from there then went outside and all but closed it. The man in front of me was suddenly on his knees and nuzzling into my crotch. I held the sink with one hand and his short frizzy black hair with my other. He was snuffling and grunting, his tongue slicing through my pussy lips and rolling around my swollen clit.

He worked my thighs open and got in under me, eating me out and pulling me open to probe deep up into me with his tongue. I was on the verge of orgasm when he got up and forced me over the sink.

The man tore at his pants and freed a short, stumpy erection. It was quite thick and stretched me open as it was shoved into me from behind.

I held tight to the sink while the islander man fucked me. My orgasm hit and he thumped me through it. I then just braced bent over like that and kept my hips tilted and my opening flared and available for him.

My husband and Steven were watching from the window beside the door. I held Paul's eyes and went into orgasm again with the excitement of being taken in front of him by a complete stranger this time.

"Ughh…ughhh.." the man on my back grunted and he powered up hard against me and held firm, his thick little cock throbbing powerfully and his cum flooding my vagina.

He was quite short for a man but as tall as me barefooted. I kept my hips tilted and my opening presented. He was still inside me and clamped to my back, his rough hands on my breasts and his fingers pinching my nipples.

"Next time I bring my friend, yes? He can fuck too?"

"Uh huh you can bring your friend," I told him. "Maybe just in my mouth though."

"Ooh yes, pretty mouth," he said. "You suck, yes? You suck our dicks?"

"Uh huh, I'll suck them. Yours and your friend's."

"Ah good girl. Very good girl," the little islander man went on.

He resumed humping me, groping my surging breasts with one hand and holding me down by the back of the neck with his other. My face was pressed to the sink and I held my husband's eyes and kept my hips flared and my opening available for this other man to enjoy getting himself off inside me. Steven had gone from the window but Jasper appeared grinning and talking into Paul's ear while clutching his shoulders and watching over one of them.

I knew Jasper could easily afford to finance our stay there on the island, but I was excited to be contributing like this. I was thinking how this islander man might even come back and forth more often with nice things for us if I could make it enjoyable for him. He certainly felt thick in me and I hoped I felt nice and tight for him, in spite of me being quite gooey and slick, the semen from his first deposit dripping down one of my inner-thighs as far as my knee.

I reached down between my legs and wiped the dribble up to my pussy. I rubbed it into my mons and split my gooey fingers over the thick shaft sliding in and out of me. The little man on my back grunted and ploughed up into me. He held firm with his cock throbbing powerfully. I caressed his heavy balls and squeezed them, just holding them lightly and feeling them pulse in my hand as his spurts of semen lashed my cervix and flooded my vagina again.

"Mmm, do you like that?" I asked him sweetly. "Does that feel nice?"

"Ooh yes, pretty girl. Loco likes very much."

"Uh huh, and you can have me every time you visit, okay. You and any friends you want to bring."

His receding dick slipped out of me and I held my pussy to stop a gush of his cum oozing out with it.

I wanted to keep his cum inside me. Where all the cum from these men belonged.

I was theirs. I was their plaything – their cum doll – and I loved it.

I did get to thinking about the possibility of falling pregnant to the little man though. I was thinking it through later that day when trying out the new bath the men had set up for me under a tree. It was too big to fit in the cabin and they were all there on the veranda with their cold beers watching the show.

I got to thinking and kind of liked the idea of having a baby to an islander man. Thinking about the lovely skin tone he or she would have and probably nice naturally dark hair, while I have to colour mine. Plus they seem such beautiful people, gentle and kind.

Hmm I liked the idea but really didn't mind which of the men ended up getting me pregnant. They all had their attractive physical qualities, different from one another but equally as appealing to me. I had a giggle imagining a boy as tall and well endowed as either Steven or Thomas. Hopefully he'll get that from his daddy. Or if it's a girl, Jasper is the most attractive with his lovely green eyes and almost pretty face.

As it turned out, none of them had gotten me pregnant yet, because my period arrived right on time the next week. It was a bad one too and I put the guys on hold for a few days, making them do it for themselves if they needed a release.

Right after my period I figured I was safe for a while too. Jasper was the first to have me of course. I was leaning over the kitchen sink with him on my back and taking his pleasure. Paul was outside on the veranda and we maintained eye contact through the open window.

"Nya fuck!" Jasper roared and slammed hard against my bottom to hold firm.

I kept staring into my husband's eyes as I was being inseminated for my first time this new cycle.

"Yeah baby that's a fucking load."

"Uh huh, feels like it," I said back over my shoulder but still didn't break eye contact with my husband.

Jasper resumed moving in me. He had been standing up but rested over my back now. He smirked at Paul. "Hey man, she said she's good to go again. Figured I'd get the first shot off into her."

"Yeah that's good, you should be first," my husband acknowledged, making me blush.

"Damn straight. Creamed her good too," Jasper said and kissed my neck. He was still inside me, still fucking me.

"Mmm but are you finished yet?" I asked him, snuggling back. "Do you have some for me to taste as well?"

"Fuck yeah you want some more!" the guy growled and continued fucking me over the sink until he was ready. Then I quickly spun around and got on my knees for him.

He gave me a nice big mouthful to swallow there with my husband still watching. It was first thing in the morning and when Steven got back from fishing he was next, taking me up to the loft and fucking me nice and deep while the others were there in the cabin listening and urging him on.

Paul waited until after lunch before taking me himself. Then Thomas took me to his bed after dinner. He still insisted his testosterone levels were best in the evening, so had been happy to wait all day.

He was certainly ready and fucked me for such a long time before finally losing it and thrusting deep into my belly and adding his deposit.

"Uh huh I can feel it," I breathed into his hair. He was on top of me, between my spread legs. I was holding my husband's eyes again. He was standing there at the end of the bed watching with his cock in his hand.

My husband spent a lot of that week or so with his cock in his hand watching me being fucked. The men had settled into the idea that the whole reason we were here was to fuck me. As soon as any of them had enough time to build up another load, I was being taken again.

I generally let them have one time each in my belly per day and as many other times as they needed, I was stroking and sucking and swallowing for them. The three younger men, that was. Thomas was strictly one a day in the evening.

The other three had already been inside me one morning when Thomas actually started kissing me. It was before lunch. This was unusual but I went with it and thrust my chest upward as he kissed his way down to my boobs.

I was lying on the couch, had been reading until he distracted me. "Mmm what are you doing, Thomas?"

He nuzzled down to my belly, lifting the skirt of my frock and kissing my shaved mons.

"Um Thomas..?"

"It's alright love, just a little taste yeah!"

"Um but all three of the others have just..!"

"Yes I know, I can smell how steamy you are from them," he said and nipped at my clit. He had the front of my panties stretched down. I could feel they were soaked. I must have been a mess.

I gripped the older man's hair and my eyes rolled as he isolated my little button and sucked on it. I lifted my butt as he stretched my panties down my legs. I extracted one leg and spread wide as he snuffled and licked into me.

"Do you like this, love? Being eaten out after sex?"

"Uh huh."

"Uh yeah so full," he groaned, peeling me open and suddenly plunging his tongue inside me. "Ooh those young men and their virility."

"Uh huh but you're virile too," I said, stroking the older man's hair as he settled to licking me out. I giggled a bit. "Mmm do you think eating that might help with yours?"

He chuckled, looked up at me with cum all over his mouth and dripping from his chin. "Maybe it will… Paul says he's been doing it for you and it's worked for him."

I giggled some more. "Hmm I think he just likes doing it now. He's at me every time after one of you other men have finished with me."

"Yeah well I've always wondered, love. I've seen this kind of kink online and always wondered what it would be like."

"Oh I see... And?"

"Yeah tastes kind of horrible," Thomas answered with a frown and he wiped his mouth on my inner thigh.

"Mmm it's not so bad when you get used to it," I told him.

"Yeah I guess," he said and crawled up the couch on top of me. He freed his cock and entered me. "Uh yeah definitely works!"

"Ahh huh huh," I moaned and bit down on my lip, grimacing against the pain until I got to used to the depth of his penetration as usual.

Thomas fucked me and filled my belly with his seed that day and was ready again that night after I'd sucked the others off, swallowing down all of their cream for my sweets.

It was getting close to my ovulation time one night when I was lying with Thomas. He had been kissing me and using his fingers to bring me to my first orgasm. He was behind me, his erection against my back. He lowered to position it for insertion but I whispered to him, "Do you want to try it the other way?"

"The other way, love?"

"Uh huh – back there," I uttered, and I positioned the narrow head against my anus. He pressed forward. It opened me. "Uhh..hh, that's um."

"Just relax, love. I'll go slow."

"Have you done this before?"

"Only a couple of times, many years ago."

"Oww! Wait! Wait!"

He pulled back, the head of his dick squeezing out and relieving the pressure. He dipped it into my pussy to get some lubrication. I held him and positioned him again. He slid back in, and I gritted my teeth against the pain but didn't stop him this time. I kept hold of his shaft and didn't allow him to go too deep but gradually relaxed my hold as he slowly moved in and out and the discomfort abated.

"That's it, love. I'm all the way in now."

"Uh huh but keep going slow for a while, okay?"

Jasper cleared his throat. "Is that what it sounds like going on there?" He peeped around the curtain.

"Just exploring new territory," Thomas said, and he held my hip and ground against my bottom, his dick fully imbedded in me.

Paul appeared beside Jasper. Thomas slowly withdrew then inserted his entire length into me again. I held my husband's gaze as the older man continued slow fucking me like that. Thomas breathed into my ear. "That's so tight, love."

"I'm glad," I uttered. "I'm glad I'm nice and tight for you like this too."

I held the sheet at my waist. I was being taken beneath it, my breasts bare and bouncing as Thomas began to lose control and hump against me. He gave a final surge and held firm, his dick flexing and throbbing, semen gushing deep into my back passage.

"Yeah cum in her arse, man," Jasper cheered. "That's so fucking sexy."

"Mmm, feels nice. It feels so deep," I said.

Thomas kissed my neck. He was still firm enough, and he resumed slow fucking me. "That's slippery now, huh?" he whispered into my ear. "Can you feel that?"

"Yes, keep doing it," I said, squirming back onto him. "Does anyone else want to?" I asked, blushing at Paul and Jasper. "You can all have me like this if you want."

Jasper stepped forward, feeling his cock through his shorts. Thomas gave another few thrusts then withdrew. He moved from behind me and picked up his clothing from the floor. Jasper stepped out of his shorts and underpants but left his tee-shirt on. He climbed over me and lay behind me. I turned my head to accept his kiss, and I arched my hips and presented myself while he positioned his cock head and entered me. "Uhh..hhh," I moaned, biting my lip and bracing as he pulled back and surged up inside me again.

Jasper settled into rhythm fucking me. Thomas joined Paul watching, and Steven appeared beside them. The sheet had been pulled aside. I lowered onto my belly with my bottom raised, and Jasper mounted my back and grabbed my two pillows, positioning them beneath my hips. I rested my head to the side watching the three men as Jasper resumed humping me. He was a little thicker than Thomas, but I was slick and open. He was surging into my arse and grinding against me, his balls slapping my pussy. Suddenly he jammed in deep and held firm, his dick swollen and throbbing.

"Mmm, that feels nice," I said, peering back at him.

"You like that, baby?" He pulled back and squeezed off with the head of his cock still inside me.

"Yes I like it," I replied shamelessly.

Jasper surged forward and bumped against my bottom again. He humped a few more times. Paul approached, feeling his cock. Jasper looked at him and grinned. "You want a turn, man?"

He nodded. "Yeah."

I blushed.

Jasper got up off me and fixed his pants while my husband mounted and slipped his cock into me. He surged forward and ground against my bottom. I peered back over my shoulder and held his gaze while he fucked me, reaching his climax quickly and pumping it into me.

Their semen was oozing from me and dripping on the pillow. I just lay there watching the older men while Steven mounted me and positioned the head of his cock at my anus. "Uh..hhh," I moaned as he entered me. "Oh, that's so deep – so amazing." I reached back and held his hip, encouraging him to press close.

"Do you like me all the way in?"

"Yes, all the way. See how deep in me you can cum, okay?"

"Yeah, go for it, Stevo," Jasper cheered. "Ride the slut, man. Ride her fucking good, eh!"

I blushed across at the men watching. My body was being jolted, Steven slapping against my bottom as his cock hit the magic spot deep inside making me scream and convulse in an intense orgasm.

Steven came fast, jamming hard and holding firm. I pressed back against him, taking his load as deep inside my bottom as I could. His swollen cock throbbed and gushed, he cried out as his body jerked spasmodically, until he had finished emptying his balls and quickly softened.

I clenched my anus as I felt him slip from me. He got up off my back, and I removed the pillows and pulled the sheet up to my waist.

"Are you okay, love?"

"I'm fine, Thomas. I'm a bit wet and messy back there is all. It didn't hurt much, though – just a little bit at first. I really liked it. Especially one after the other like that, then Steven hitting the special spot!"

# Paul

I had completely lost it. I had no control over what any of these guys were doing with my wife anymore. That next afternoon Loco showed up with fresh supplies and he had another islander with him, a man about his age and quite overweight.

We all unloaded and carted the supplies up to the cabin, then got to drinking beer and having a bit of a party. Justine was more conservatively dressed than usual, in a pretty little floral dress that buttoned up the front. It was quite short and often flashed her white panties, but other than that it kept her covered.

The two islander men were often checking her out and chuckling between themselves. Justine was smiling and blushing at them. I came back from the toilet just after dinner and saw them taking her down towards their boat.

"It's alright, man, they're just gonna collect their fee," Jasper said and winked.

I didn't challenge him. I just walked off into the forest and made my way down to the boat. I crept aboard and had a look down into the cabin where my wife had the fat islander's cock in her mouth and the other one's stumpy dick sliding in and out of her arse.

The fat guy looked up at me just as he pulled my wife's head close and bucked. He groaned loud as he shot his load in her mouth. She swallowed in audible gulps while moaning and still sucking on him. Loco then resumed humping her and was soon squashing her flat on a bunk bed and blowing his load up her arse.

I backed up the stairs and went for a walk along the beach for a couple of hours. When I got back to the cabin I found Thomas sitting on the veranda and Steven asleep in a hammock. I went in to find that Jasper had my wife up in the loft and they were sleeping cuddled together.

I woke once during the night and listened to him kissing and fucking her.

Justine approached me working in the garden that next afternoon. We'd hardly spoken all day.

"Hey, can I talk to you?" she asked, standing back a bit.

I nodded and took a breath. There was a rock nearby. I motioned to it and Justine sat. I rested back on the ground in front of her. "Hey," I said.

She took a big breath too. "So, I was thinking I'd like to start sleeping with Jasper each night for a while, if that's okay with you?"

"Oh right." My chest had tightened. "Did he say something?"

"Um, yeah, I know he wants to." My wife stretched, flexing her hands in front, grimacing and blushing quite deeply. "It's just that I've been checking my timing with my cycle, and I'm pretty sure I'm about to ovulate soon. Probably later this week, would be my guess."

"Oh right." I was blushing now.

Justine grimaced some more. "You other men can still have me from behind, or I'll suck you off anytime you say. It's just that Jasper knows and he wants to be the one."

I swallowed hard. "The one, huh? Like to get you pregnant."

"Yes." Justine nodded. "I really want him to be the father, Paul. We can still raise the child as ours of course, but with the way things have been here, it's only natural that we should let him get me pregnant, don't you think?"

"Only natural huh? Fuck!"

Justine slipped to her knees and moved close. "Please?" she asked sweetly. She claimed my hand and put it under the skirt of her dress. She pushed my fingers into her cunt. It was gooey and open, her inner thighs sticky. "That's his. He just keeps grabbing me and fucking me, Paul. We were watching you from the kitchen window just now and he took me right there and filled my pussy with his sperm again. It just feels so right that it's his inside me at the moment."

"Yeah, well, I'm fucked if I know what to think anymore," I shot back angrily. I don't know where it came from but I'd suddenly had enough. I looked squarely at my wife. "If you really want to have the fucking arsehole's baby, he can fucking have you."

I strode off leaving Justine gawking open-mouthed after me. It felt good at the time, but when I eventually returned to the cabin that night, I found Steven and Thomas playing cards and the sound of Jasper fucking my wife up in the loft again. She was crying out with each thud of the cot against the wall. He let out a loud groan and with one final bang the bed stopped thumping.

"Yeah baby, get that fucking baby batter into you eh!"

"Uh huh, fill me up again," Justine uttered. "Mmm don't pull out yet," she cooed sweetly.

I turned and slunk from the cabin, walking off into the forest night again.

# Epilogue

It had been a full three months on the island before we returned home. I had been through quite a few ups downs and peaks of extreme angst, but overall I had passed the days and nights somewhere between excited for my wanton wife and absolutely defeated and cuckolded into submission by the other men, and alpha-male Jasper in particular.

Then there was the scandal. Justine was pregnant of course. She had been stranded on a desert island with four men and come home pregnant.

The talk was favouring me as her husband having accidentally gotten her, without having any birth control for protection. The rumours and inuendo were favouring Justine having been shared around by all of us men.

The fact that Jasper, Thomas and Steven were regularly visiting us and often staying the night fanned the flames of excitement around the rumours. They would visit and fuck Justine. She remained horny all through the pregnancy and the guys wanted to be included.

The baby was born healthy and it wasn't obvious who the father was. We named her Cynthia. She took over all of Justine's time and energy for a while but before long the guys were coming around quite regularly to fuck my wife again.

It has just gone two years since the plane-wreck and Jasper has the others all onboard for another trip to the island.

"Mmm I'd like to," my wife moaned into a kiss. "Wouldn't you, Paul? Just the five of us again and we can take our island baby along to see where she was conceived."

"Oh yeah, and to make her a little brother or sister, I suppose?" I asked back into the kiss.

"Mmm okay, if you insist," my wife uttered and bit my lip. "You kinky husband you!"

** The end **

Printed in Great Britain
by Amazon

25183493R00131